Twisted Mountains
Tall Stories From Britain's High Places

little peak press

Twisted Mountains – Tim Woods

First published in 2021 by Little Peak Press

www.littlepeak.co.uk

Copyright © Tim Woods 2021

Tim Woods has asserted his rights under the Copyright, Designs and Patents Act 1998 to be identified as the author of this work.

Foreword copyright © Helen Mort 2021

Edited by Jo Allen

Unless otherwise stated, all photography by Tim Woods and Heather Dawe. Osprey photograph (front cover) by Iain Poole (Pixabay).

Design and production by Rhiannon Hughes
www.theyorkshirewordwright.co.uk

A CIP catalogue record for this book is available from the British Library.

ISBN: 978-1-9160812-3-9

Printed and bound in the UK

This book is dedicated to everyone who
has ever been up a mountain with me.

Contents

Foreword

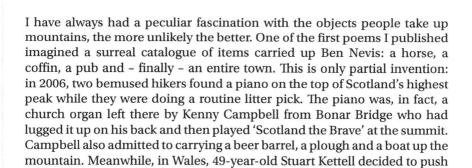

I have always had a peculiar fascination with the objects people take up mountains, the more unlikely the better. One of the first poems I published imagined a surreal catalogue of items carried up Ben Nevis: a horse, a coffin, a pub and – finally – an entire town. This is only partial invention: in 2006, two bemused hikers found a piano on the top of Scotland's highest peak while they were doing a routine litter pick. The piano was, in fact, a church organ left there by Kenny Campbell from Bonar Bridge who had lugged it up on his back and then played 'Scotland the Brave' at the summit. Campbell also admitted to carrying a beer barrel, a plough and a boat up the mountain. Meanwhile, in Wales, 49-year-old Stuart Kettell decided to push a Brussels sprout up Snowdon with his nose to raise money for Macmillan Cancer Support. It took him 4 days and 22 sprouts to finish the task and climb over 3,000 feet on his hands and knees.

I love these stories because they are whimsical, improbable, testament to our arbitrary feats and utter resilience, our stubbornness and sense of joy. But they have a metaphorical resonance for me too. The narrator of my poem about Ben Nevis concludes sadly that the one thing they wish they could keep close has been left behind: "I couldn't take you with me. Not a step." So much of our mountaineering and adventure discourse is about freedom, wilderness, leaving our humdrum existence behind. The Great Outdoors as Great Escape. We might think we go climbing or running or kayaking or swimming to 'lose ourselves' and become immersed in the present. But I'm increasingly interested in the things we carry with us into the hills – our egos and fears, our mixed motives. My interest has been amplified, perhaps, by the arrival of my son in 2019. Since pregnancy, I have been carrying him before me in the mountains, first as a hidden presence, then as a bump that attracted curious stares when I scrambled up Munros, then as a wriggling baby strapped to my chest or cradled in a backpack. Nowadays he scampers in front of me, bribed by Smarties, but his presence dictates every adventure, every route chosen or ignored or deemed impossible or saved for later.

Foreword

I am drawn to Tim Woods' writing because it explores what is carried, what is lost as well as what is found, placing mountain adventures in the context of complex (and often far from admirable) lives. Put simply, I love these stories. They are full of surprises and revelations, but many of those revelations are the stuff of everyday life: razor-sharp observations of all that is anticlimactic, frustrating, bittersweet. Here are voices we don't usually hear from in the hills – bikers and landowners and jilted lovers, lads from Fort William plotting a crime that will make their fortune. In 'Oology', a conservationist takes matters into their own hands with a brutal flourish. In 'Offcomers', a wealthy woman tries to buy the view that possesses her. Elsewhere, in 'Two Hundred and Eighty-Two', a dad is left with young twins while his partner goes AWOL in the Scottish Highlands. Mountains become sites of revenge and murder, cynicism, greed and thwarted ambition. Here are characters who love the natural world, but understand or embody the contradictions in our approach to it. Musing on bees and wasps in 'Oology', the protagonist says wryly:

"The margins are exceptionally fine: one set of yellow-and-black stripes will get you an online petition, another will get you a rolled-up newspaper."

In 'First Ascent' – a harrowing tale of a life given meaning through climbing – tragedy is offset by dark humour: "The problem with patience is you never know how long you'll need it."

Tim's writing is far from ordinary – his characters live and breathe, his prose is witty and evocative – but he charts ordinary moments with acute clarity, the non-events that can define a life. In 'An Exmoor Carol', the protagonist changes his entire mode of being, emboldened by the wild spirit of the moors, but nobody really notices. So often, these stories chart the role of mountains in our attempts to make connection and find meaning. The task is impossible: the mountains do not care for what we graft onto them. In this, Tim's work reminds me of what I've always loved about M. John Harrison, his eye for the miraculous and the mundane, how the two converge and make truth stranger than fiction, fiction more real than life. There is tenderness and compassion in Tim's portrayal of character, but it is tempered by an anti-romantic awareness, a sense that we all make our own choices. One of my favourite stories, 'Like Father, Like Son', charts a fractured relationship between man and boy and how it is mediated and threatened by the father's desire to put the outdoors first. He wants to share mountain landscapes with his son, but sometimes that in itself comes between them. He reflects sadly:

"The passion wasn't there; that unshakable thirst for the outdoors, a willingness to do absolutely anything for a day in the hills. He'd nurtured it from an early age, in case it wasn't passed on genetically, but he had failed."

Failure is a consistent theme in *Twisted Mountains*: both landscapes and people fall short of what is demanded of them. It is achingly perceptive. It is also dramatic and compelling: 'Local Hero' begins with the unforgettable line: "What would you do if you found a body on a mountain?" The writing also gives us moments of transcendence. Even characters who aren't easy to like are capable of profound appreciation. In 'Offcomers' the eastern face of a fell is "scorched through with thick black shadows... a shifting show of shadow puppets". And though these stories offer us a clear-sighted account of what burdens us in the hills and what we burden the hills with, there are moments of escapism too:

"She shared pictures from the first few summits, but soon stopped. They were her memories. Why share them with people who hadn't made the same sacrifice?"

I have said too much. These stories speak for themselves. Each one is a breath of fresh mountain air.

Helen Mort

1 Ysgolion Duon

I'm out before sunrise. I need to be up there before anyone else. If I'm going to do this, I have to be alone.

Leaving the bike in Bethesda, I set out for Cwm Llafar. Past the bunkhouse, over Afon Cenllusg, and from there it's simple: follow the Afon Llafar upstream. I soon hit a steady pace. The air is fresh, rinsed clean by the overnight downpour, and the river is full, much higher than on our first walk together. Our first day together; we'd only met the night before. I can remember every detail of that day. That's why I'm going up there, why I'm following the same route. He'll know why I did it, of course he will, but doing it at that exact spot – our spot – it sends a message, doesn't it?

Maybe Carnedd Dafydd wasn't the best choice for his first walk. Craig was unfit, he never did any sort of exercise. Apart from one thing, of course. We did plenty of that. But the Carneddau are tough for anyone, let alone someone on their first proper hike. And it was after a very late night, too. We didn't leave the nightclub until three, and didn't get to sleep until... well, a lot later than three. I should have suggested to the others that we did something easier, or maybe waited for a day when it could be just the two of us. But Craig insisted; he wanted to come with me, to meet my friends. I even suggested we turn back at Cwm Moch, when he could hardly breathe, could hardly get himself up again after the drinks stop. But he refused. He wanted to get to the top, he said. It took us five hours, and another three back down.

It was his decision. I never forced him to do anything he didn't want to.

I'm faster today, of course, despite the pain in my ankle from that fall two weeks ago. And even though my rucksack is much heavier than usual, I don't stop at Cwm Moch, or head to the summit cairn. Instead, on reaching the plateau of Carnedd Dafydd, I go to the edge and look over, down into the vast, dark-grey corrie of Ysgolion Duon. It's my favourite place in Snowdonia, right at the top of a very long list.

I set down my pack halfway along the ridge, right by the edge and then search for the spot where Craig and I had lunch that first time. And, a few months later, where I proposed. Yes, I proposed to him. But I can't find it at first. I thought it would be easy, a location seared onto my mind. Is it hidden by the snow? There's still a bit about, tiny patches hidden in the shadows. To let out a little tension, I kick over one of the small piles of stones that people leave beside the path. I think about destroying them all, but there isn't time. I need to get on with this, or I won't go through with it.

There it is: a large triangular stone, half-covered with bright orange lichen, very close to the edge. I can't remember why we sat there on that first day. Probably to get some space, a moment to ourselves. But it became our stone. That's why I made him come back up here to propose. It's why I'm here now.

So, here I am. There's nothing else to stop me. But I can't, I'm not quite ready. Instead, I go and gaze into the corrie. It's four hundred metres to the bottom, but looks like far more from here. I'm going to make a hell of a mess.

Not just yet, though. There's no one about, I don't need to rush. I wish I'd made some coffee, but there didn't seem any point. The plan was to get it over with as quickly as possible, not pootle about up here. But now I wish I had made some. I could do with a coffee.

I can understand why my friends had their doubts, right from the start. Craig and I were hardly a typical match. Nothing in common. Both twenty, but that's about it. In every other way, we're complete opposites. The outdoor enthusiast and the local DJ. No one could understand what we saw in each other.

Correction: they understood what I saw in him. Everyone fancies the DJ, don't they? It was what he saw in me that defeated them. He could have anyone, why has he picked her? I don't blame them, I thought exactly the same myself. Every day we were together.

They could have tried, though. They could have made more of an effort. But that's the problem with university clubs, especially the outdoor societies: they're elitist and insular, indifferent to anyone who isn't as passionate as them about their sport. 'Your friends don't like me much.' That's what he said, after that first walk. I told him it wasn't true, even though I knew it was. Jerry and the lads all laughed at him. Behind his back, but close enough to be heard. They mocked him for being unfit, for being too scared to go along the ridge to Carnedd Llewelyn. 'It's not that far, come on.' Maybe not too far for them, but it was his first walk. Carnedd Dafydd is hard.

The girls tried a bit, I suppose, but they weren't much better. No one asked him anything about himself, anything about his music, or what it was like being a DJ. They just talked about mountains, climbing, biking; which summits they've ticked off. Anything that didn't include him. Maybe it wasn't deliberate, but they could have been more thoughtful. Only Anja, my best friend, made any real effort to get to know him.

Good old Anja.

It was so different when I was with his friends. They were much kinder. They all had that same thought at first, I know – what's he doing with her? – but they didn't say it, that's the important thing. And they included me in their world: the music, the clubs, the drugs. They looked after me, too, always making sure I had a lift to and from whichever club Craig was playing that night. He couldn't, of course, because once he had loaded up his car with all his precious records, there wasn't room for me. God, he loved those records. Almost as much as I love the mountains.

And it was wonderful. I adored being one of the cool kids, just for once. I'd never heard of Northern Soul, but Craig told me everything I needed to know. About floor fillers, floaters, the whole history of the scene. It was his dad who had got him into it, and Craig loved it even more. 'I'm keeping it alive for future generations,' he always said. And it's true, people went crazy on those nights, I mean properly crazy. They never left the dance floor, barely even paused for breath, all moving to the music my boyfriend was playing for them. And I was in among them. I'm in with the in-crowd... that was one of the songs he played. Anja loved that one too, once she started coming with us.

We couldn't always go, of course. He usually played Friday and Saturday nights, and that's when the society has its big trips away. It wasn't possible to do both, not every weekend. So if there was something important in the calendar, that was it. I couldn't always go with Craig.

Correction: I didn't always go. I could have chosen him over the mountains, if I'd wanted to. So what happened was partly my fault, too. It wouldn't have happened if I'd always been there. Not so soon, at least, and probably not so often. I should have made the sacrifice. Put Craig first. But I didn't, so I have to share some of the blame.

Our stone is cold when I eventually sit down. Me too: I'm shivering. It's chilly, even though the sun is now pushing through the early morning haze. I really do wish I'd made coffee.

It didn't come as a surprise when I found out. You don't get unsexy DJs, do you? Even when they're a bit overweight, like Craig. Drugs, music, girls, that's what it's all about, isn't it? They swarmed round him even when I was there, so if I wasn't there... well, what did I expect? I knew he would sleep with someone else eventually, that's part of why they do it. But as long as he came back to me, I didn't let myself mind. And he looked genuinely sorry when I found the condom wrapper in his pocket. A different brand to ours.

'It won't happen again,' he said. There was no 'I promise,' though.

We still had some good times, even after that. He came with us on a couple more walks, despite the way the others treated him. Not anything big, but he was there on Yr Eifl, on Moel Hebog. At Easter, he even drove us, just the two of us, to the Llyn coast for a weekend away, one when he wasn't DJing. He'd planned it as a surprise, because I was stressed about my final exams. So he definitely cared about me. I think he even loved me, in a way, but not like I loved him. Not even close.

It was during that weekend away that I decided to propose. It seems ridiculous now, but I really thought it might make him think twice on those nights when I wasn't there. I thought a ring might rein him in. People said it was too soon, but people always say that, don't they?

'You're too young,' said Anja.

'He's too young,' said his friends.

'OK, if you really think it's a good idea, just be prepared for when he says no,' said Dad.

Thanks, Dad. Really supportive.

That's why I brought him back up here. He wasn't keen on the walk, of course, but I managed to persuade him. I thought it would make it more significant, if I did it in the same place we'd had lunch on our first day together. Here by Ysgolion Duon. I wanted it to be special. I even bought champagne. Actual champagne, not the cheaper stuff. He seemed genuinely pleased when I asked, maybe even a little flattered.

Me? I was relieved. You're not supposed to be relieved, are you? Only propose when you know they'll say yes, isn't that what people say? But as he hugged me, all I could think was that from now on he wouldn't sleep with any of the women he met while DJing. Or at least not so often. It's not the most romantic reason for proposing, now that I think about it.

A fell runner goes by, staring straight ahead. They never look at the floor, do they? How do they not trip? What would happen if she fell up here, all on her own? There's no one coming up the path behind her.

She could be the last person I see today. No one else is about.

I think I could have lived with it, if it only happened on the club nights, when he was away. I could have turned a blind eye, so long as he always came back to me.

But my fiancé and my best friend? I couldn't ignore that.

I should have realised earlier, of course. I was so, so stupid not to see it. Craig and Anja were always chatting together, or laughing on the sofa when I got home from the library. I was actually pleased, can you believe it? So stupid that I didn't notice when she stopped coming on the society's weekends away. Thank goodness one of my friends gets on with him, that's what I thought. It never occurred to me both of them knew that I'd be away. That they would have the flat to themselves.

I don't know how long it might have gone on if I hadn't slipped on Crib Goch. That was another foolish decision on my part. It was too wet; no one else wanted to go out, but I insisted. Only Jerry would come with me, and then only so I wasn't up there on my own. It wasn't a serious fall, just bruising, nothing broken, but in the car Jerry said I should go to the hospital, just in case. He was adamant, now I think back, kept going on about it. I didn't realise he was trying to delay me from getting home. And when he dropped me off, he wouldn't come inside. He wouldn't even look me in the eye. So I guess Jerry knew all along, too. Maybe they all did.

I don't blame Jerry, though. I don't even blame Craig. It's not actually all that glamorous, being a DJ in Bangor, playing ancient records in poky little pubs to people the wrong side of fifty. And far less important than he thinks it is. But it's still more exciting than being the events secretary for a university walking society. And there's far more glamour in sleeping with Anja than there is with me. She's funnier, sunnier and much, much prettier. Far more glamorous. So no, I don't blame him. But I do hate him.

It takes quite an effort to drag the overloaded rucksack to the edge of the vast greyness of Ysgolion Duon. But I manage and, seconds later, Craig's treasured record collection is crashing down it, each one chiming a glissando as it shatters into a million tiny pieces. Their last musical performance. In among them are fifty-year-old classics and much-sought-after rarities, many of which are impossible to replace. Together, they're worth close to eight thousand pounds. Craig never tired of telling me how valuable they were, or how long it had taken to put his collection together. I wonder when he'll notice all the sleeves in his bedroom are empty. Soon, I hope.

And her? We're no longer best friends, of course. We're still flatmates, but only because I haven't found anywhere else to live yet. I'll move out as soon as I do. I did consider doing the unthinkable, and pushing her off a ledge somewhere. 'It was an accident, it was windy, it was slippery!' But I'm not sure anyone would believe me. I doubt she would ever have come out with me, anyway. And it would have been an excessive punishment. Just about.

17

Still, she'll miss her bike. That Stumpjumper was a twenty-first birthday present from her parents which, by a neat coincidence, also cost close to eight thousand pounds. I don't expect it will take Bethesda's teenagers very long to find a valuable, unlocked bike on their patch. Nor will she be able to claim it on her insurance, because I cancelled that yesterday. Never reveal your passwords, Anja. That's the first rule of online security. Everyone knows that. And don't sleep with your best friend's fiancé, either. I thought everyone knew that rule, too.

I lie flat on my stomach to enjoy one last look at the shining fragments of North Wales' finest Northern Soul collection. There is a tinge of guilt about the mess, but not a huge one. I feel a bit better already. And the sun's out fully now, so I've stopped shivering. I'm feeling better all over, in fact. Better than I have in weeks. And with my rucksack now much lighter, I decide to make a proper day of it. I'll head over Carnedd Llewelyn, down Y Braich and into Capel Curig, where I can finally get my cup of coffee.

Craig will miss those records. He loved them as much as I loved him.

Almost as much as I love the mountains.

2 The Stravaiger

Hiding in plain sight. That's how Deano Thomas describes it as we sit in the corner of the Nevis. I like the sound of it. Like the sound of his scheme altogether.

'It's this big shooting lodge, out in the middle of nowhere. Been working there six months now. The guests, English wankers, they always leave at three, straight after a massive fucking lunch, and they never get back till five or later. Which gives you two hours minimum to sneak into their rooms, take whatever you find and get the fuck out. They go straight from shooting to drinking, they won't notice anything's missing till much later.'

I nod slowly. I'm already thinking through my own plan for how this could work. 'Why not do it yourself?'

'I can't, can I? It needs to be someone they won't recognise.'

'What if I get caught? I'm kind of on my last warning with the police, y'know?'

'That's the best bit, wee man. By the time the police arrive, if they even bother going out there, you'll be hiding over at the bothy. I promise you, no one'll think to check some wee shithole out in the hills.'

'You sure about that?'

'Aye, and if they do, all they'll find is you on your lonesome. Whatever you get, you stash it out on the moor, remember? Even if they do go to the bothy – and they won't, trust me – they'll never search the moor. It's fucking massive. You wait two days, until they've given up checking the trains, then bring it all back here.'

'And no one else'll come looking for us?'

'No chance. It's miles from anywhere. You have to get a train in, there's no roads, and people only go there to climb the mountains. Just take a sleeping bag, enough food for two days, and chill. Enjoy the fresh air. If anyone turns up, you're admiring the scenery. Like I say, hiding in plain sight.'

'Aye, sounds good to me.'

'You bring everything back here and I'll sort it from there. Sixty-forty split.'

'No way, man. Fifty-fifty or I'm not doing it.'

'Sixty for you, you daft wee prick.'

'Oh, right. Aye, sounds good.'

I think for a minute. I don't know Deano all that well, but well enough to know he'll stitch me up given a quarter of a fucking chance.

'I'm bringing Gav along, mind.'

'You sure about that, wee man?'

I can understand his surprise. Most people don't want to spend two minutes with Gavin Durie, never mind two days, and with good reason. He's a violent crack addict with a long habit and a short temper. There aren't many situations where you'd willingly have Big Gav tagging along, but robbing a house where every other bastard has a shotgun is one of them. He isn't my friend, you understand. What we have is more of a dealer–junkie kind of vibe. And Gav is one of my best customers.

'Aye, I'm sure,' I tell Deano.

'Your choice. You'll have to split your share with him, though.'

'No problem,' I smile. Deano's not gonna know how much we get, so he can't know what his share should be. And if he doesn't like what I give him, he can take it up with the local crack-addled psycho. He's the daft wee prick, not me. I raise my lager and he raises his, the age-old mark of a done deal.

But on the journey down to Corrour, I'm wondering if I've made a wee misjudgement. We almost miss the train because Gav wants to stop at McDonalds – three of the big fellas he finishes off, all by himself – and it's slow getting there. There isn't much to chat about either. It's hard to make small talk with a crazed hooligan in a sour mood. What you been up to, Gav? Beaten anyone senseless for no fucking reason lately? No, better to leave him staring out the window. I don't want those eyes on me, those eyes have seen many terrible things – all things their owner took great pleasure in doing. Best left alone is Gav. So I'm happy enough when we get off at the station. Normally I get nervous before a caper, but it's a relief to be off that train.

'Mind that, Gav, we're four hundred metres up out here,' I say, nodding at the metal sign by the tracks to prove I'm not making it up. He doesn't reply. Fair enough, not everyone's into the heights of stations, but I'm already sensing it'll be a long two days.

We take the path from the station, just as Deano instructed. It's long enough but eventually we reach the house - and the back door is open. Each bedroom's unlocked too. These rich bastards have way too much trust in their fellow man. And rich is an understatement. We fill my backpack with watches, phones, rings. Even Gav cracks a wee smile when we get to the last room and there's piles of money there, just lying about. On the bed, on the table, even by the khazi. We grab it all and sneak out.

No one to be seen downstairs, so we follow the route Deano drummed into me: take the burn until you reach this big bastard of a hill, then right towards the loch. And hey presto, just visible in the twilight, there it is. The bothy. Before we get to it, though, I head onto the moor to stash the backpack. Like Deano said, criminal mastermind that he is, that's our insurance if someone comes out here, the key to making sure we're not caught with crimson-coloured hands. It also means he can't sneak out here and steal it from the bothy, which I wouldn't put past him. Gav'll know where it is, naturally, but if he's planning to fuck me over there's nothing I can do to stop that. No one else will find it, though, not in a year of searching. Deano was right: this place is huge. Hiding in plain sight.

'How much d'you think?' I say, rooting through the backpack.

'Dunno. How much do these sell for?' Gav asks, picking out a gold watch.

'No idea, big man, Deano said he'll sort that side of things. There's at least four grand in cash, mind.'

'We should just keep that, no?'

'And how do we explain that if someone turns up? Why would anyone bring four grand out here? Fuck all shops that I've seen.'

Gav says nothing, just shrugs.

'But,' I say, peeling off a few purples, 'I reckon we deserve a wee something for our efforts so far, eh?'

'Aye, nice one,' Gav agrees, putting his share in his back pocket.

I pick out a skull, a deer or some other poor bastard that has to live out here, and mark the spot. It feels a bit morbid and I hope it isn't tempting fate, because you don't need to encourage the forces of darkness when you have Big Gav Durie for company. To prove my point, the next thing I know there's a blade at my throat.

'If you try to rip me off, or even think about it, I'll cut you. You and Dean Thomas. Understood?'

'Absolutely, big man, clear as crystal. Thought never crossed my mind.'

'Is that the bothy?' he asks, calm as you like, before he's even put his knife away.

'Aye, must be.'

'Bit small, isn't it?'

'It's only for two days.'

'What are we gonna do for two days?'

'Look at the stars. Enjoy the great outdoors. Fuck all else to do.'

'Did you bring any gear with you?' he asks.

'Nothing, big man. Nada.'

'Nothing? You're a drug dealer, aren't you?'

'Aye, but... I'm allowed a weekend off, no? Sorry Gav, I didn't think.'

He shrugs again, and heads around the back while I take a look inside. Gav's got a point: it's small. Just two wee rooms, one left, one right. In the right one there's a fireplace and a wooden sleeping platform, but not much else. No TV, no PlayStation. Gav comes in as I'm about to check the other one.

'Where's the toilet?' he asks.

'There isn't one. You have to shit outside.'

'Are you serious?'

'Aye, man, there's the wee spade, you have to cover it. C'mon, it's nature. Embrace it!'

Gav doesn't reply but when he comes back, I sense he isn't embracing it to the full.

'Did you see a shopping bag anywhere?' I ask. 'With food in it?'

'Nope. Just deer shit and grass.'

'Fucking hell, Deano's not left us any food? He said he was gonna leave something.'

Gav doesn't reply, doesn't offer to help with our lack of food situation at all. He just lays down on the wooden platform and closes his eyes.

'Two days without food, big man. What're we gonna do?'

Again, my partner in crime doesn't respond. He isn't much in the way of company, it's fair to say. I decide to sit outside. It's dark and cold, but I don't want to chew the fat with a hungry crack addict about to go cold turkey.

He comes outside much later for a piss. After washing his hands in the burn – for a crackhead, he has fair respect for the basics of hygiene – he sits down by me.

'What would you eat right now, if you could have anything?' I don't know why I ask him about food. It isn't a good idea, poking a hungry bear. But fair play to him, he makes an effort.

'Fish supper, with extras. What about you?'

'Sushi, man, a nice bit of sushi.' I lick my lips at the thought of it. 'You like sushi?'

'Do I look like a man who eats sushi?'

I laugh and Gav laughs as well. I wonder if it's the first time in his life.

'What're we gonna do, big man? I can't last two days without food.'

'You'll have to go back to that house in the morning,' he decides. 'See what you can find.'

'Me? Why me?'

'Your plan, your problem.'

I consider pointing out it's kind of a shared problem, but Gav isn't all that keen on nuance and reason. More a black and white sort of guy. And before I can think of anything else to say, he's up and inside. Conversation over. I stay outside a bit longer, even though there's still a few of the midge bastards eating me alive. At least they're getting their supper tonight.

I'm up late the next day. Not sure how late because all those expensive watches are out on the moor, but the sun is up and doing its stuff. There's no sign of Gav and I'm happy to leave it like that for as long as possible. A man like that, with no food or drugs inside him... well, he isn't gonna be in one of his sunnier moods. But thankfully he stays inside all day, except for the odd piss. It's only when the sun is on its way down again that I spot another human being. The old girl is definitely coming our way. With tension shooting up my spine, I go inside to wake sleeping ugly.

'Gav, man. Gav! There's someone coming.'

The big man comes outside, looks at where I'm pointing. We watch for a couple of minutes, but I already know exactly where she's heading.

'Get rid of her.'

'How?'

'Don't care. But you get rid of her or I will.' He heads back inside. I reckon Gav's solution is gonna be a wee bit more permanent than mine, so I wait for the old girl to reach the bothy so I can tell her to fuck off, loud enough for Gav to hear. She greets me with a big old smile, her grey hair all over the place, and she's lugging a pack twice her size. She doesn't have boots on either, just leather sandals with socks underneath. She's a crazy old dame, there's no mistaking that.

'Sorry, but you can't stay. We were here first.'

'First rule of the bothy, lad, there's always room for one more.'

'Aye, but we were hoping for a bit of peace and quiet, y'know? My pal and me.'

'A Brokeback Mountain sort of trip, is it?'

'Nah, I didn't mean that, it's just...'

'Don't worry, I'm only staying one night. You boys take one room, I'll have the other. Can't say fairer than that.'

I head in to tell Gav, just in case he didn't hear. 'She won't leave.'

He doesn't say anything, just gets up and heads outside. I follow, keeping a safe distance. I hope this isn't gonna be messy, because the police might not bother coming out here for a few stolen watches, but I reckon they would for a murder. Or two.

'Like my friend here says, you can't… what's that?'

I was only inside for two minutes, but the old girl has already set up a stove outside and got a pan bubbling away on top.

'Venison stew, and I've brought plenty. You never know who you'll meet in the hills. Would you like some?'

'Aye, sounds good.' Gav sits himself down, staring at the food, hunger proving a stronger itch than the need to kill someone.

'There's water boiling for tea as well,' she says, pointing to another wee stove. A minute later she's spooning brown goop onto pan lids and I can hear my stomach gurgling. It isn't sushi, but it still smells good.

'Are you here for the Munros?' she asks, handing us a lid each.

'They're the mountains, right?' says Gav, wolfing down his stew.

'That's right, lad. That's one of them, one of the biggest.' She points with her fork to the big bastard behind us. 'Ben Alder. Are you planning to climb it?'

'Nah, we're just hanging out here a bit,' I mutter. Gav gives me a stare, a warning not to share our private business with a newcomer – even one that's feeding us.

'Hiding out at Ben Alder cottage? Just like Cluny Macpherson!'

'Is he a friend of yours?' Gav asks.

The old girl laughs at him, which isn't the greatest idea, but fair dues, Gav takes it well enough. Doesn't punch her into next week. 'You could say that. I must have read *Kidnapped* at least fifty times.'

'What about yourself?' I ask, keen to avoid Gav dwelling on the idea of kidnapping. He doesn't need any encouragement, that boy.

'I'm not interested in mountains, laddie,' she replies. 'No, I'm ticking off the bothies. My ambition is to spend a night in every bothy in Scotland, walking between each one. A stravaiger, that's what they call the likes of me. Wandering from one place to the next as the mood takes us. So tomorrow I'll be heading for the next one. I haven't decided which, that's part of the beauty. Anyway, that'll do me for today. I'll bid you both good night.'

She scrapes the last of the stew from her plate, gulps her tea and heads inside.

'What d'you think?' I ask Gav when she's inside.

'Why would anyone sleep out here if they didn't have to?' he asks.

'Don't ask me, big man. But I mean, should we let her stay?'

He shrugs. 'If she's off tomorrow morning, it should be OK.'

He gets up and makes towards the bothy as well. I follow this time. The risk of being murdered by Gav is less daunting than battling with those midge bastards.

Next morning I'm up early, and decide I might as well have a crack at the big beast of Ben Alder. I try to convince Gav to come, but he isn't having it. He even watches me leave for the mountain to make sure I don't head for our stash out on the moor. It's as if he doesn't trust me, which I'll admit is a wee bit hurtful. I don't go to the top of the mountain, can't see the point, but I sit for a while to think. It's going to plan so far, but there's a whole day before we head back, and I don't have faith in Gav's good mood lasting that much longer. At least the old girl will be gone when I get back, one less problem to worry about. Aye, she'll be well on her way by now.

But a couple of hours later, as I return to the bothy, I realise I've made a terrible mistake. I can hear Gav from a way off, shouting and screaming and hacking away. My heart lurches at the thought of what he must be doing to her, and it's all my fault. As I creep around to the front of the bothy, my worst fears are confirmed. Gav is standing there in just a vest and trousers, knife in hand, blood all over.

'I caught a fish!'

'You fucking what?'

'A fish! I caught fish in the loch. The woman, the one with the stew, she showed me how. I caught a fish!'

It's kind of beautiful, seeing this great hulk of a crack addict beaming like a bairn on Christmas morning. But I can't quite believe he hasn't killed her as well as the poor wee fish dude. 'Where is she, big man?'

'At the burn, rinsing the fish out. We're making another stew, we picked wild herbs as well.'

As my head spins with the idea of Big Gav as a rustic cook, she comes back. And she's in one piece rather a thousand tiny ones.

'How was your walk?' she winks at me.

'Alright, ta. I hear you two've been fishing?'

'We have, lad, your friend is a natural. An expert at gutting them, too.'

'Aye, that I can believe.'

'Here you go.' She hands Gav the fishies and the big man chucks them into the pan. Again, I can't quite believe my eyes as he takes a wee pinch of herbs and sprinkles them in, all delicate.

'Keep stirring it, laddie, it won't do if it sticks.'

'Like this?' Gav asks her.

'That's it, nice and slow. And you boy, you can get the rice cooking.'

We sit there, cooking our tea on wee stoves like Boy Scouts, and soon enough the feast is ready. It's hard to eat though, because the midgie bastards are swarming and I have to bat them away the whole time. The old girl has the same issue, but they don't seem to be bothering Gav. I can't blame them, I wouldn't want to drink his blood either, given all the shite that's running through those veins. Most of which I sold him, I have to admit.

'That was great,' says Gav with a massive belch.

'Aye, not too shabby,' I concur.

'It always tastes better when you've made it yourself,' offers the head chef. 'And a fine meal needs washing down with a fine whisky.'

She leans down and picks up a bottle of whisky that was hiding among the pans. Good stuff, better than the piss I usually drink. She swigs heavily, then hands the bottle to Gav.

'Ta,' he mutters.

'I'm guessing you're from Fort William,' she smiles. 'Correct?'

Gav's good humour vanishes in a flash. 'How do you know that?'

'Partly your accent. And you've got the letters "FW" tattooed on your left shoulder.'

'You've got me there,' Gav replies after a long pull on the whisky. 'Corpach.'

'It's a fine old town,' she assures him. 'With a wonderful bothy not too far away. Slàinte!'

'Aye, whatever,' Gav says, finally handing the bottle to me. I make sure to get a good few mouthfuls before handing it back. It's not certain I'll get another turn with those two around. But the whisky gets passed round again as she tells us about all the bothies she's been to. One where you can pick fresh mussels from the shore. One where a stag pushed open the door during a blizzard and joined her for the night. One where she had it away with a stranger, a story that I did not want to hear. When we finish the first bottle she pulls another one out of her Tardis-like rucksack, and even Gav is laughing away by the time we've polished that one off. It's amazing what getting out of Fort Bill can do for a psychopath. That and a litre of whisky.

'I've spent half my life wandering the world, laddies, looking for something better. And let me tell you this: there isn't anything. This country is the finest there is. To Scotland!'

She drains the last of the bottle and almost falls over backwards. I can't believe there's nowhere better, but then I've only seen a couple of other places, so I'm not in a strong position for a long debate.

'Aye, to Scotland,' I say.

We both look over at Gav. Now, Gav's not exactly what you'd call a nationalist; he hates everyone equally, no exceptions made for his fellow countrymen and women. But there must be something in the air tonight because the big man nods and cracks another wee smile.

'Aye, alright. To Scotland.'

'I'm heading west tomorrow, laddies, you'd be very welcome to join me? There's supposed to be a grand wee bothy at the foot of Loch Treig, one I've not been to yet.'

Gav catches my eye, suddenly all serious again. 'Nah, you're alright.'

'Aye, we might stay another day,' I add, trying not to sound too cagey.

'Fair enough, fair enough. Then I'll bid you both a good night.' She gets up gingerly and heads inside. Gav and me wait a few minutes more.

'I could get into this bothy lark,' I say.

'Aye, it's alright, no?' he replies.

'Maybe we can head to that one with the mussels one time, what d'you think? Now you're a master with the old wild herbs.'

'I don't like seafood,' Gav mutters, then heads inside. Fair play, it's not for everyone. Maybe I'll go by myself. Or maybe I'll go overseas, somewhere hot, add to my somewhat limited set of passport stamps. I'm gonna have plenty of money to spend in a few days. I follow the big man inside, already dreaming about where I might head.

The sun's already setting himself up for the day when a kick on the foot wakes me up.

'Time to get moving,' Gav mutters.

'Aye, give us a minute.'

I pull on my jacket and head outside, splashing some water from the burn onto my face to wash away the worst of the hangover. It makes fuck all difference, though, my head is still churning. I can just make out Gav's shadow in the gloom and follow as he strides out across the moor. He's moving fast, the big man can clearly handle the whisky better than me, which isn't a surprise given what else he shovels into himself. Twenty minutes later, with the sun now dancing about, I find our skull. And nothing behind it.

'Shit. It's not here, big man.'

'What d'you mean?'

'I mean, it's not fucking here. I left it behind this skull. It's gone, Gav.'

He comes over and checks. Like I'm gonna lie to him.

'Someone must've taken it,' I say, stating the fucking obvious.

'Who? There's no one out here except us and...'

He turns and runs back to the bothy. I can't keep up but I'm not even trying, I know what we'll find. The old girl's rucksack is still there, in the corner of her room, but of her there is no sign.

'How did she know where it was?' Gav asks, staring at me in a way that doesn't fill my heart with gladness.

'She must've watched us stash it from over on that big bastard of a hill. Or Deano must've tipped her off, they'll be in on this together.'

Gav nods slowly, mulling over this unfortunate turn of events. 'They're dead. Both of them.'

'I'm with you there, big man. No excuse for that kind of behaviour.'

It takes us half a day to walk back out along what must be the longest fucking footpath in Scotland. Gav stops to stare at a signpost on the way, studying it with a concentrated look on his face.

'Loch Treig, isn't that where she's heading?' he asks.

'Aye, big man, but I think she might've spun us a wee yarn there, no?'

Gav nods, taking the disappointment pretty well. At least that's how it seems, right up until he puts his fist through the window of the wee restaurant on the station. The station guard gives us a suspicious look, sitting as we are next to a smashed window, and Gav with blood and cuts all over his hand. But he decides not to say anything. Fair enough, it wasn't his window.

Gav doesn't speak either, not until we're halfway back to Fort Bill. 'She's got some nerve, hanging about with us and then robbing us.'

'Aye, hiding in plain sight.'

'What's that?'

'Doesn't matter.'

We reach Fort Bill and I'm keen to make a sharp exit, no point hanging about. 'See you around, then Gav. And sorry about all this. Bad luck, eh.'

'Aye right, nice try. You're coming with me.'

I hope we're not heading to his dad's place, because the apple didn't fall too far from that fucking tree, and Mr Durie Snr lacks the patience and even-handedness of his eldest son. But no, we're heading straight to the flat of the grandmaster himself, Mr Deano Thomas, Fort Bill's soon-to-be-dead, or as close to it as counts, criminal mastermind. I want to run, but there's no point. As Gav has proven already this morning he's got a fair turn of speed for a lumbering crack addict.

Deano doesn't look that pleased to see us, but then no one wants an angry Gavin Durie on their doorstep. 'You twos back already? How did it go?'

Gav doesn't answer him, not with words anyway. I stand back as he leaps forward. Deano falls backwards while asking, not unreasonably, what the fuck is going on, and when they're halfway along Deano's hallway I take my chance and leg it to the station and the next train south. On the way I throw away Gav's blade, which I took from him last night, risking my beautiful wee face in the process, but I felt I owed Deano that much. My luck is holding and I manage to jump on the train heading south just as it's about to pull away. The doors shut and I breathe out, as this gives me at least two hours' head start on Gav or Deano, or both of them if they work out what's happened before killing each other. I'm still nervous as the train curves south through Spean Bridge, Roy Bridge, Tulloch, because you can't trust anyone these days, not even family, not always. But she's there, sat on the bench at Corrour, with my rucksack next to her. She gets into the same carriage and I shake her hand, fair play, she's put in a cracking performance, credit where it's due.

'You been waiting there all the time?' I ask.

'No, laddie, I decided to wait on the other side of Loch Ossian. To be on the safe side. Quite literally. I watched you and your friend depart, then had a wee dram in the restaurant at the station. A nice bit of beef as well, beautifully done it was.'

'Lovely,' I reply, suddenly feeling hungry myself. 'I couldn't believe it when you stayed another day, though. That wasn't what we agreed. A bit fucking risky, no?'

'I was enjoying myself. There's nothing like a bit of fresh air, besides your friend isn't half as scary as you made out,' she chuckles. 'And you boys did well, very well. We'll take it to my associate as soon as we reach Edinburgh. Fifty-fifty split, as agreed?'

'Aye, sound,' I reply. 'Or maybe we can get a wee bite first, when we get there? I'm starving, Nan. It's not an easy job, babysitting Big Gav for three fucking days.'

'Fair enough, laddie. What takes your fancy?'

'I'd be happy with a nice bit of sushi,' I tell her.

'Sushi? Raw fish and seaweed? Best left for the otters, lad.'

'Aye, you're maybe right there, Nan. You're maybe right.'

3 First Ascent

It's dark, as black as pitch. Too dark to see anything. I wave a hand in front of my face. Nothing. Blind? I don't think so: there are tiny stars dancing before my eyes. Blind people don't see stars, do they? I slap a cheek to check if I'm alive, then pinch it to be certain. Not dead; that's something, I suppose.

Carefully, I move myself upright, using just my arms. There's no feeling in my legs, not yet. I lean forward and slowly, very slowly, reach for them. They're soft to the touch. Don't feel like legs any more. Wet, too. I can't tell if it's mud, blood, or a mix of both. The right one is especially bad. Thank God for the darkness, hiding what I surely don't want to see.

Behind me feels a little more solid and I shuffle myself against whatever it is; wood, sandbags, I'm not sure. There, better already. I'll be comfortable while I wait. How long for, though, that's the question – and one I can't answer. It can take an age to dig these things out once they've collapsed, longer than it takes to build them. I know, I've done it enough times. All I can do is wait.

I close my eyes – not sure why, I still can't see anything – and head for the Highlands, the place I've been escaping to these past few months. Back to where it all started. My first climb...

Norm's the foreman. More senior, and there's a fixed hierarchy in the shipyard – one that people like me can't challenge. I never ask him about climbing, but always listen keenly when he and the others are talking about their weekends in the mountains. One day, he spots me lurking nearby.

"You coming with us, then? Nothing like the Ben for your first time out.'

I nod, hoping it isn't a cruel joke. Scotty, who's standing nearby, has a scowl on, furious he hasn't been asked as well. We take the train up after work on the Friday, my pockets full with wages. Until we reach the pub, at least; by next morning, they're half gone. Mam'll give me grief, that much I know.

Norm tells me halfway up that the route is called Càrn Mòr Dearg, but I barely hear him. Three, four times, I think I'm a goner, certain I'll fall. I can't believe they've taken me up something like this on my first time.

Later, back in the pub, Norm admits he wanted to test me, to see how I reacted. You can tell straight away if someone's a climber or not, he says. He also tells me we'll be doing a 'proper' climb tomorrow. How much harder can it get? I spend the rest of my wages to block the thought out, crashing on the pub bench in a fug of beer, nerves and exhaustion.

We set off before the sun is up, and Tower Ridge seems simple enough to start with. Norm says we won't need the rope until later, so I keep it coiled around me as I follow him up, watching how he moves, where he holds on, where he pushes up. It's easier this second time; it already feels natural. And if I'm scared, it passes too quickly to notice. I'm too excited at being part of the gang, being away from Glasgow. As I come off the ridge and onto the summit, I want to scream, to tell the world what I've just done. But Norm is already coiling up the rope, getting ready to head down. 'Wait until winter, we'll come back and do it properly,' he mutters.

Mam is furious about my wages, and she has every reason to be – half of them should have gone to her. But I wouldn't have missed it for anything. Norm was right: there's nothing like the Ben for your first time.

There's a fierce buzzing in my right ear. It must have been damaged when the shell hit. Painful, but at least it's a change to all the other noise out here: the rain, the rats, the screams, the gunfire. Worst of all is the chatter, the constant bloody chatter. And the poems. God, they're awful. Write them if you must, but don't make me listen to them. That's one of the things I love most about the mountains: the quiet. There's space up there to hear your thoughts. I have a bit of that now, though, while I wait to be found...

Norm barely speaks when we're climbing. He's too focused, always concentrating. He doesn't say much the rest of the time either, but even less when he's on the rock. And when he does speak, it's always about climbing. Nothing else interests him.

We travel up in a storm, a bad one, but Norm is pleased. Storms clear the skies, he says. And, as we set out for Bidean next morning the conditions are perfect. Fresh snow, bright skies, no wind. He leads the way, but lets me cut some steps in the snow. He even remarks that they aren't all that bad, which is praise enough from him.

The steps are too good, in fact: we're down by mid-afternoon, far too soon on a day like this. I could climb all day, and suggest we attempt another route. But Norm won't have it: never push your luck in the hills, he says. If you have a good start, make sure you have a good finish. He says a lot of things like that. Experience, you see.

We go to the Clachaig once we're down, and drink while waiting for others to drift in. Some are old, some young, some tall, short, stocky, wiry; but all with one shared obsession. Their tales get longer as the night does the same, the near misses getting closer to death and disaster with every telling. For some of them the drinking seems more important than the climbing, but it holds little interest for me. I let them talk, my mind already outside among the ridges and peaks that surround us. Routes on every side, calling me, tempting me. I twitch and fidget all night, desperate to be out there.

'Relax, son, there's plenty of time,' Norm whispers to me. 'Plenty of time.'

The problem with patience is you never know how long you'll need it. Fridays never came around quickly enough for me, but at least I knew they would eventually. Now, though, I'm stuck, waiting for someone to dig me out, but not knowing when it will happen. Or even if it will happen; not everyone gets found, not always quickly enough anyway. All the waiting around is just one of the things that drives me mad out here.

Scotty drove me mad too, especially once he started coming out with us. No, it was more than that: I couldn't stand him. Not at first. Why? Because he was better than me. I was good, but he was a phenomenon. It infuriated me. From the start he was fitter, more courageous, with a longer reach and stronger limbs: he could hold a position for as long as he needed to complete the move. He had confidence, too. There was no flapping about on his first time. And routes that took me ages, he raced up on his first attempt. I couldn't bear it. It still gets to me now, even after everything that's happened. And plenty has, since we were sent out here.

Plenty today, even. I still can't see my legs but I can feel the pain rising up through them. I don't know how bad they are, and I don't want to. It's daft, isn't it? Here I am, too afraid to touch my legs, after climbing some of the hardest routes in Scotland without so much as a flicker of fear.

Hardly a flicker, anyway. I had one or two moments...

Coire Gaothach scares me shitless. A thousand feet of snow and ice clinging to a vast bowl of black rock. I can't take my eyes off it, I'm lost in its enormity, unable even to think about where, or how, to start. It feels like the rock is staring back down at me, daring me to even try it.

We came up late last night and slept in the forest, so there was no forewarning of what we would be attempting. I've heard about it from the others of course, and plenty of times, but nothing can prepare you for seeing it for the first time. My left leg has the shakes, twitching like a mad thing, and we haven't even started. I think about lying, telling them it's the cold, but there's no need: they are too busy arguing to notice. Norm wants to take an easier line, one he's done before, but Scotty is desperate for something new, something he can put his name on as a first ascent. Something that will get him noticed. They're close to fists, and my leg is properly going now, the fear really starting to bite. The cold, too.

They can scrap all they want: I need to move. We agreed Scotty would lead, but I'm not waiting any longer. I take one last look at the wall above me, swing my axe into the ice and move. Sure enough, they both shut up and follow. I'm a good way up before I even notice my leg has stopped shaking. That's just how it goes sometimes.

Even the old boys in the pub in Tyndrum are impressed: the eastern face of Beinn Laoigh is a noteworthy name in anyone's book, especially a relative beginner like me. I'm the toast of the bar, don't have to buy a single drink all night. Scotty is sick with envy each time someone reaches over to clink my glass. That just makes it all the sweeter. He needs putting in his place.

I shuffle back again, trying to make myself a little less uncomfortable. I can feel splinters of wood jabbing me, but that's the least of my worries. I need to shift the weight off my mangled legs, but it doesn't help much. And freezing water is now pooling around my arse. The rain over here is something terrible, not that a Scot can complain. But the flatness is the worst. That's the first thing Norm noticed when we arrived in Belgium. Too fucking flat, this place, he said. He was right, as always. This country is empty, devoid of character. There's no depth to it, nothing on the horizon to mark yourself against. It's featureless, pointless; why would anyone fight for it? I'd defend Scotland to the death, but this place? I can't understand why we're here. Yet here we are, scrapping for a few feet of land or a hill a bit nearer the river to look out from. They're not even hills, not in my eyes. Just bumps in an empty land. That's what marks Scotland out: our scenery. Wherever you go, there's a shape to the land. Especially on Skye. You'll find proper mountains out there. Or so I've been told, anyway...

I save for months for the trip, putting a little aside from my wage packet each Friday. Scotty does the same. But we arrive to fierce, driving rain. We can hardly even get the tents up.

'You can't climb basalt in this,' Norm says. 'Too dangerous, there's no point being daft.'

We manage a few low-level routes between the worst of the weather, but nothing that justifies the cost of getting up here. Nothing that comes close to satisfying me. We don't even set foot on the Cuillin. So Scotty and I make a pact on the train back to Glasgow: we'll return at the first chance. Just the two of us next time: we're good enough to climb on our own now. Neither of us says as much, not out loud, but Norm is starting to slow us down a little. We're better than him. He's holding us back.

I don't expect I'll make it back to Skye. Not now. Still, I've got a better chance than Scotty. He's not going anywhere, not all of him anyway. They'd have to find the missing bits first, and that could take a while. Poor bastard. I don't even know if I'll make it back to Scotland. But even if I don't, there are seven routes that will forever hold my name as their first ascent. Scottie finished on five. He'd be absolutely furious about that.

The buzzing's stopped, and I can hear shovels scrape at the earth, voices barking out orders. Muffled, but I can tell they're speaking English, so we haven't been overrun. I can't tell if they're trying to reach me or someone else, or even if that's what they're doing. Sometimes they rebuild the outer wall first, to stop the whole trench collapsing in. They'll find me eventually, but however long that takes, it'll be too late. I know that now. There've been times, too many of them, I've told other lads that everything will be alright. I've held their hand and promised they'll be home soon, even as their blood coats us both. You can't lie to yourself, though.

I'm ready for it, I think. I've lasted longer than most. Longer than Norm or Scotty. But I don't want to be here when it happens. Mam always warned me that I'd die out on those bloody hills, and I don't want to disappoint her. Not again.

I'll go to Ben Arthur, one last time. Now that's a hill worth fighting for...

It's my favourite right from the start. Love at first sight, but I'm hardly alone in that; the Cobbler Club even stole its name – although that causes more than enough arguments. Many a night the old boys argue over which name is right. Some hate its English nickname, but others says it's earned the right to stand out from all the Bens. I never take sides; the names mean nothing to me. All that matters is the climbing.

The three of us sometimes head up in the week, after our shift ends. In the summer, the days are long enough to take the train up and get three hours of climbing in. That's plenty for the Cobbler, and it's simple enough to come down in the dark. We sleep at the station and get the first train back. I never risk it alone – being late means getting the boot – but Norm, he's a foreman, he can get Scotty and me out of any sort of bother.

The southern ridge is empty this evening, not a soul about. The rock is dry and grippy after the day's warmth and I'm climbing better than ever, almost walking up. Norm and Scotty, they can't keep up. I can hear them below, in the distance, but their voices soon fade away. I'm alone, nothing but the mountain and me. I jam a foot into a crack, steady myself, and turn around to absorb the view, to take in every peak that surrounds me. The sun is dropping but its light lingers, shimmering on the loch in the distance.

From nowhere an eagle swoops past, inches from my face. I almost fall off in surprise, thankful for the wedged foot that keeps me in place. Its bright yellow eye watches me, considering this strange creature that has broken into its space. I want to explain, to tell it why I'm here, but before I can think of a reason, it's gone, flying along the loch that stretches all the way to the Clyde.

4 No Experience Necessary

I park the van by the path that leads onto Brownsey Moor. One by one, they clamber out. My team. My crew. My regulars. My gang.

My volunteers.

Officially, they are the Upper Dales Conservation Society. Informally, they are the 'Dirty Weekenders'. Privately, I consider them the people for whom society has failed to find a better use every Wednesday, Saturday and Sunday. And, from among them, I must select a deputy project leader. For our masters at head office down in London have, in their collective yet still infinitesimally small wisdom, decided that by the end of this month all project leaders, i.e. underpaid fools like me, must appoint someone to help them fill out the endless streams of health and safety paperwork we receive (from head office), prepare annual, quarterly and monthly budgets (for head office), take part in weekly project updates on Zoom (with head office) and organise and document regular training opportunities for volunteers (upon which head office insists, whether the volunteers want them or not). And all of this time-wasting is because head office has decided, without any consultation (despite those weekly Zoom calls), that we are no longer a conservation organisation. No, we are now – as every bit of correspondence proclaims, in bright green letters and missing a hyphen – a 'People First Organisation'. Whatever that might mean; no one has actually explained it to me, although someone down there created a wonderfully complex diagram that would, they promised "mainstream the engagement concept fully to all relevant stakeholders". The diagram included lots of tick-boxable terms like "volunteer experience" and "inclusivity", but nothing so vulgar as "tree" or "habitat" or "endangered species". The buzzwords have usurped the buzzards.

What head office *didn't* create was a budget line for this new role, so whoever steps forward will be doing it for even less than I am paid, i.e. nothing. Their reward is nothing so vulgar as money, but rather soul-nourishing concepts like "personal growth" and "skills development" and the chance to work for "a stimulating, creative organisation" and various other platitudes that landlords are not commonly known to accept as rent. Oh, and applicants need a clean driving licence, plus a willingness to give up three weekends each month. For free. Why people aren't axing down my door for this golden opportunity is a mystery. And there's no money to advertise the position either, so I must appoint from within the ranks now milling about trying to decide who will carry which tool to the work site.

Pat is the obvious choice. My oldest volunteer in both age and years of active service, he's always the first out of the van and quick to take charge. There he is now, barking at the others to be careful with the expensive new spades and to get a bloody move on. Late fifties, military background, he's organised, efficient, resourceful: all qualities that a good deputy requires. There's nothing he doesn't know about conservation work either, from building a drystone wall to reflooding a wetland. He's my hardest worker and knows more about Yorkshire than I ever will.

The problem is that head office have specified the need for a "people person". And while I am not exactly sure what that means either, I am certain that Pat is not one. "Miserable old bastard" is the phrase that most people plump for. He only talks to others when there's something to criticise: their work ethic, their inability to fell a tree in two swipes of an axe, or simply that they're in his way. He verbally strikes down anyone who complains that it's too cold or dark or windy, and woe betide the volunteer who downs tools for a tea break a second too early. Pat rarely joins us for tea breaks, seeing the intake of hot liquids as one of humankind's most unforgivable flaws.

Another hurdle is that deputy leaders need a first aid certificate, and Pat doesn't really believe in first aid. It is, in his view, for "for moaners and whingers" and anyone with an injury should "bloody well get on with it". He's coming over now, with a Kelly kettle in one hand. It's not an obvious choice of impromptu weapon, but you can't be too careful with Pat.

'We'll need to pencil in an extra day next week. Wild Boar Fell. Footpath's been damaged, just after the second junction – you know where I mean. Bloody little hooligans.'

I know exactly the spot he means and exactly how it got damaged, but I'm careful not to promise anything. I detest footpath work: it's arduous and tedious and most sections that need attention are high up on the fells, which is a long way from anywhere when you're carrying heavy tools. It's thankless, too; you spend a day sweating and toiling to improve about two square metres of path, and no one ever notices. Actually, that's not quite true; occasionally a passing hiker will point out the stones we've just spent many back-breaking hours putting in place aren't level, or that we're ruining the natural beauty of the Dales. People, eh? The countryside would be so much pleasanter without them.

Pat lives for such work, though, and his dedication to keeping the footpaths of the Yorkshire Dales in fine fettle, come rain or shine, is a blessing, for me and for the ungrateful ramblers. Pat does all the organising, which leaves me free to look after the other volunteers. And trust me, they need looking after. Especially Addy.

'Just gunna sit here, right? Won't do nowt. You'll still sign my forms, right?'

I have to keep a particularly close eye on Addy, especially on days when we're clearing scrub or hacking away rhododendrons – any task that involves making a fire, basically. Likes a good fire, does Addy. In fact, it's his unhealthy fixation with them – specifically the starting of them – that means he's legally required to spend two days each week volunteering with us to repay a small part of his considerable debt to society. Credit where it's due, he hasn't set fire to anything for weeks now, but the embers of love have never fully died down. He can sit and watch a fire for hours, even the small one that heats our kettle. That's all he does, whatever the task; I've yet to see him swing a billhook in anger. To describe him as demotivated would suggest there was motivation present at some point in the past. He is – and I say this with due acknowledgement to pots and kettles of every shade and hue – a lazy bastard. In lieu of work, Addy, with his mad stare and hair from the Chewbacca range, sits on the grass and daydreams of his pyromaniacal past. We have an unspoken agreement: if he doesn't go within ten feet of the matches, I sign his forms and pretend he did his bit. Needless to say, he's not really got what it takes to be my number two.

Josie, by contrast, is positively overflowing with beans.

'Shall I make tea? Does everyone want tea? I'll make some anyway, just in case.'

A warm, kindly ex-hippy, she never has a bad word to say about anyone. Rarely a coherent one, either, the legacy of a youth spent doing mushrooms, acid and whatever else she was offered. She certainly adds colour to our gang, not least because she has the fashion sense of a Victorian prostitute. Today she's wearing a crenulated velvet dress in a shade of pink that can only be described as "extremely". I have often reminded her that frilly museum pieces aren't ideal for practical conservation work, but, like Addy, she never does any actual work. Instead, she spends each day organising the tools in order of size, then cleaning each one meticulously with a small lace handkerchief. While talking to it. Which is fine because I never get round to cleaning them, but the demands placed on a deputy leader are slightly more extensive than polishing bow saws and asking how their day is going. So she's out too, which is a shame as she would help considerably with hitting our gender equality targets.

By default, Stephen qualifies as the normal one.

'Ring ouzel spotted in Dartmoor. Might drive down there after. First one this year.'

He's a dedicated twitcher and checks the various apps on his phone every few minutes to see if anything interesting has flown in. He once drove all the way to Cornwall for a grey catbird, watched it for two minutes, then drove back. The following week he treated us all to a minute-by-minute account of his trip down the M60, M6 and M5, including every service station he stopped at along the way. I couldn't tell you which he liked the most, having stopped listening halfway through his detailed review of the available snacks at Charnock Richard.

Stephen's passion for wildlife would, in many ways, make him the perfect deputy for a conservation organisation. Unfortunately, his views on people from other countries are far less friendly and most definitely not in keeping with our inclusiveness policy. We are, remember, a People First Organisation, but Stephen puts white British people like himself first, and quite a long way ahead of all others. For him, Brexit was like birthday, Christmas and Kristallnacht all in one. He'll drive five hundred miles to watch an avian migrant and march twenty more against the human kind. Which means he's also out of the running. He's lovely otherwise. Honest.

As the gang sets about resetting the flagstones high up on the breezy slopes of Brownsey Moor, I realise there's a couple of newbies with us today, who somehow sneaked into the van without my noticing. Two teenagers who, I am willing to bet, are here as part of their Duke of Edinburgh's award. That is the only reason teenagers ever choose to spend their weekends hanging around with people like us. Volunteers that age usually slouch about with faces like a stagnant pond, but these two actually seem to be enjoying themselves. The girl is tall and smiley, while the boy is earnest, spotty and so far out of her league that no amount of listening to and agreeing with her every word is going to get him so much as a sniff. Amazingly, they seem to have somehow met with Pat's approval. There he is, scrutinising their handiwork and not swearing at them. He must be in one of his better moods.

So cheerful is he, in fact, that he even joins us for the mid-morning tea-break. And why not? It's a sunny spring day, one perfect for being outdoors. Such is the general sense of bonhomie that I don't even step in when I spot Addy poking the fire beneath the kettle. I can't bring myself to stop him, he looks so at peace with the world. Besides, he can't do any significant harm as the local gamekeepers have already scorched the heather into huge black rectangles, ruining what would otherwise be a stunning landscape. As we each find a spot to sup among the charred vegetation, Josie hands out her home-made brownies, proudly informing us that they are vegan, nut-free, lactose-free and gluten-free. Sadly they're also taste-free, although not sawdust-free judging by the texture. After hiding mine beneath a sheep poo, I ask the young newbies if they're enjoying themselves.

'S'alright, thanks.'

'Yeah, s'alright.'

Clearly they're not the chattiest pair. Maybe that's why Pat's taken to them.

'So, so sorry I'm late, but I'm here now, how can I help, what can I do?'

Last as always, Dom jogs up the slope wearing a broad smile and expensive-looking waxed trousers. Now, Dom would make an excellent deputy. He's cheerful, friendly and the fact he's somewhere approaching sane puts him way ahead of the field. He doesn't lack self-confidence either, the kind of person who chops up an apple and calls it fruit salad. And he has a real passion for the Dales, talking loudly and constantly about how much happier and healthier he is since moving up from Shoreditch. Yes, Dom loves it so much that he spends at least three days here each month. He'd love to spend more, of course he would, but simply can't be away from his web-something-or-other company for very long. Heaven forbid, Dom.

He once showed me the very article that had persuaded him to make the move. It was one of those double-page spreads you find in the weekend supplements, all flowery adjectives alluding lyrically to the innate nobility of rural life: how the daily commute becomes an invigorating stroll along a sunlight-dappled field margin, rather than an hour on the Tube with a stranger's arse in your face. You know the sort of thing, I'm sure. I read the article with great interest. Interest that they'd chanced upon one of the four sunny days we had that year to take their photos (which included a sunset over Malham Tarn, a mere thirty miles away). Interest that the writer failed to mention the traffic jams that clog up Swaledale most Friday evenings as people like Dom arrive from elsewhere in stupidly oversized cars. Their description of houses as "affordable" was interesting, and clearly relative to salaries paid in places a long way from here. The reasons they listed for living here were also interesting: generous roadside parking came first, followed by the "acceptable" strength of the broadband. Next came the quality of local schools, average time to the motorway and the outstanding £100-a-head meals in a restaurant that isn't even in the national park. The astounding beauty of Swaledale just snuck into the top ten.

The house they featured – the one Dom bought, naturally – was certainly eye-catching. A four-bed detached cottage perched halfway up the fellside, with whitewashed walls and a flourishing kitchen garden. The photographer had done an excellent job, but could have saved his time, of course – I would have gladly provided my own humble snaps of the village Dom and I now share. I have plenty of pictures of my end-of-terrace abode, with its crumbling façade and intermittent roof slates; or perhaps an image of the Swale in spate, followed by one taken moments later of it chundering through my living room after running straight off the fells that are stripped bare by the four-legged, woolly-backed locusts that are found on every hill around here. That most recent flood was, in its own small way, good for the local wildlife: the dampness and mould that set in beneath my floorboards attracted a family of rats who have refused to move out since.

Yet, despite his Shoreditch stylings and nauseating wealth, I like Dom. Certainly more than the rest of them. I make my way over to raise, tentatively, the subject of the deputy leadership vacancy. Pat blocks me off before I can reach him, though.

'That work on Wild Boar Fell I mentioned, it'll need two extra days at least. There's plenty that needs doing up there.'

'OK, I'll take a look at the diary, see when we can fit something in. Maybe in the summer.'

'Don't be ridiculous, man, it'll need to be before summer. Can't have crowds traipsing all over it in that state. Bloody morons.'

Pat doesn't have a lot of time for walkers.

'Right, I'll have to look at the budget, see if we can stretch to more work up there.'

'Make sure you do.' Pat nods sharply, which is his way of signifying that I am dismissed. 'You two'll come, I take it?' This is addressed to our two newest members, who both nod enthusiastically.

'Aye, we'll be there,' says the girl

'Aye,' confirms her admirer.

'Good, good,' says Pat.

And there, unnoticed by everyone except me, is that rarest of sights, less common than a footpath free of banana skins and orange peel: Pat with a smile on his face. It only lasts half a second, but it's there as he contemplates having two fresh minds into which he can pour his love for and knowledge of all things footpath.

As the last dregs of Josie's moss-flecked tea are swilled down or tipped discreetly away, Pat leads his two young disciples back up the hill while the rest of them return to their preferred positions – whether working hard or doing nothing. Once they've distributed themselves sufficiently far away, I rummage in my pocket and pull out my rolling kit. Project leaders aren't supposed to smoke on tasks – fire risk, health risk, bad example, blah blah blah – but if I lie right down in the heather then no one can see me. Before I'm even halfway through its length, though, the girl comes running over. I sit up and listen as she frantically utters the words that no project leader ever wants to hear.

'There's been an accident.'

I pinch out my ciggie, head spinning furiously. Terrible things, accidents: the paperwork involved is almost unimaginable. I know already that this evening will now be spent in the office, filling out forms and hastily changing the dates on risk assessments that haven't been glanced at since the last incident (Addy, Grinton Moor, severe burns). I follow her quickly up the hillside and the others join us, no doubt hoping for a bit of blood and gore.

Awaiting us is a scene so terrible that I very nearly vomit.

There, on the grass, is one of my brand new spades, handle snapped clean in two, blade bent at a right angle. It cost ninety-five pounds – approaching half our annual equipment budget – and has seen active service for less than an hour. I won't be able to replace it either. The director of operations informed all regional offices that there is no budget left for new tools this year. I can't remember if the email came through before or after her ten-day fact-finding mission to South Africa (we are all still eagerly awaiting the fact-filled report).

'Really sorry, it just snapped,' mutters the boy, who is sitting on the side of the path, where – and I cannot quite believe my eyes – Pat is putting the finishing touches to an extremely neat-looking bandage.

'Daft bugger cut his hand on the blade. Nothing serious; it won't need any stitches.'

Next to Pat is a sizeable first aid kit, much bigger than the official project issue pack that contains little more than a few plasters and out-of-date antiseptic wipes. He catches me admiring it. 'That? Bought it last week. And

I've been on the course as well. Bloody waste of time; I knew it all already, and plenty more besides. I should've been teaching them. Anyway, I assumed you'd get around to making me as your deputy at some point, so thought I'd get myself trained up in the meantime. No point waiting for you to get around to it.'

'We were trying to move one of them big stones,' the girl explains sheepishly, 'but Pat told us you should use a crowbar for moving stones. Not a spade.'

'We'll pay for the damage, promise,' says the boy.

'Reckon that o'er there's a curlew,' mutters Stephen.

'Of course there'll have to be changes to how things are done around here,' Pat interjects.

'Shall I make more tea?' offers Josie.

'I'll do the fire,' insists Addy.

'So, so sorry, everyone, but I've got to take this call,' says Dom, smartphone already to his ear.

'Aye, definitely a curlew. Don't usually get 'em this high up.'

'There's more brownies too!'

'More footpath work, for a start. That's the priority round here, not drystone bloody walls.'

For a moment, it's all too much. They are too much, each and every one of them. I slump to the heather, exhaling deeply. Can I really live with Pat as a deputy leader? Will I be able to cope with him ordering me about? I should be the one deciding what gets done and what doesn't. He's right about one thing, though: there will need to be changes. Top of the list is an end to his night-time excursions onto the moors to vandalise perfectly good footpaths, simply to ensure a steady supply that need repairing. I followed him up Wild Boar Fell last week to confirm my suspicions, and watched as he spent two hours diligently dislodging stones, breaking up steps and clogging up culverts. All with as much care as he took when we installed them last spring.

I retrieve my unfinished cigarette while I decide what to do, to hell with fire risks and bad examples. As I search for the lighter, I spot Dom, my only realistic alternative to Pat, running back down the slope, miming someone typing on a keyboard and shrugging his shoulders apologetically as he departs to do something far more urgent and well paid.

'Come over here a minute,' Pat barks at me, already displaying a distinct lack of respect for the chain of command. 'And put that bloody thing out.'

He leads me away from the group and puts a hand into his jacket pocket.

I wonder for a moment if it's a gun, and he's decided to clear his way right to the top. And whether I'd really care if he did. But instead he hands me a bundle of rolled-up twenties.

'This is to replace the spade. Don't even think about refusing it.' (I wasn't.) 'It was my fault, not theirs, I should have shown them how to use the crowbar.'

'Thanks, Pat. That's very kind. I'd have been waiting a while for head office to send us more cash.'

'Oh, don't you worry about them, leave them to me. Bloody morons.'

'Eh?'

'Heading down there next week, aren't I. Told them I want to speak to them in person if I'm taking on an official role. Said they were busy, but I wasn't having any of it. If they've got money to fly around the world, they've got money for new tools. Fact-finding mission my bloody arse. I'll show them.'

Slowly, I begin to see the qualities that Pat could bring to this role. A vandal he may be, but is he really doing any more damage than the walkers who are incapable of staying on the paths, no matter how wide we make them? Or the 'green laners' whose vehicles leave deep ruts across the delicate moorland? Or the gamekeepers who'd burn the whole lot down if they could, anything to keep their fat, feathered goldmines happy? If nothing else, the thought of Pat bulldozing through the egos and suits in London is too much to resist.

I offer my new deputy a hand and, once he's given it a firm shake, I use it to pick up the broken spade handle. Addy can have it for his fire. I know for a fact he adores the fumes that are given off by burning varnish. He'll be over the moon, in more ways than one.

And that's what really matters. We're a People First Organisation, after all.

5 Local Hero

What would you do if you found a body on a mountain?

I just stared, because I'd never seen a dead person before. I knew he was dead because he wasn't moving, but it was more than that, it was his head, tilted at a right angle to his body, that's how I knew, heads are never in that position, not working ones anyway. After I finished my joint I crept over. I don't know why I crept, it's not like I was going to surprise him, but it seemed like the right thing to do, respectful I suppose, then I knelt for a closer look. His face was grey and the eyes were open. The whole thing gave me the shivers, I don't mind telling you, and I wondered how long he'd been there, because we, if that's what you say when one of you is dead, we were a long way from the main paths. I don't like the paths, I prefer to be by myself in the mountains, so I stick to the bits where no one else goes. Anyway the dead guy was lying in a stream and I wondered if he'd fallen against one of the rocks and that had killed him or if his head had twisted when he fell, or maybe he had a heart attack but you don't close your eyes if you have a heart attack, that's something I heard once, maybe I read it, but I don't know much about it to be honest. Anyway, I sat a little distance away to give us both a bit of privacy, and took out another of my ready-mades while I decided what to do, but a couple of puffs in I realised I was annoyed. With him. I'd been coming to the Cheviots on Christmas Day for years, although not the Cheviot itself, I don't like that one as much as the others, I never have, too many people about, so I come to another one, I'm not saying which, but like I said I've been coming up here for years and never seen a soul, although whether he still counted as a soul is something else I don't know much about, either way he'd interrupted my day and I resented it. I like the loneliness, being alone with my thoughts. I wondered for a moment if he'd had the same idea, but when I had another look I could see his eyelashes were frozen, so he must've been here overnight, maybe days, just lying there without anyone knowing, which is possible – you don't get many people coming up here in winter, especially not to these hidden valleys, cloughs some people call them, but I just call them valleys. He was a problem I could have done without, I have enough of them already with my boss at the factory and with money or lack of it and with the people that call themselves my family. So I thought about leaving him for someone else to find but like I said there's not many that come to these parts so I couldn't count on that happening. I could have called someone but I didn't have my phone with me, I never bring it out here, no signal no point, and the nearest farmhouse was half an hour's walk away and there was no guarantee there'd be anyone in, a lot of people visit their family on Christmas Day, most people in fact, it's only loners like me that head into the hills on our own. I wondered for a moment if his family were as bad as mine, maybe that's why he was up here, but whether it was or it wasn't, I decided I couldn't leave him, so I finished my joint, and headed down to the farmhouse.

The woman in the house, I've no idea if she was a farmer or not, a lot of them round here have sold up and moved on, so they're not really farmhouses even if that's what people call them, she invited me in, kind of her, but I said it's fine I'll wait outside. She said she'd ring the mountain rescue and I told her they weren't needed because he was definitely dead, but she reckoned they were the right people to call anyway and I didn't argue because I'd rather them than the police. I'm not a big fan of the police and they don't have all that much time for me either, that's just how it is, so I told her where he was, and she seemed to know, so maybe she was a farmer and not someone who moved out here, because not everyone knows the side valleys, not like I do. A few minutes later she came back with a cup of tea and said she'd spoken to them and because it was Christmas it might take them a bit longer, but they'd definitely go up there tonight, so I said thank you very much and I wouldn't take up any more of her time. And then she did something really nice, something no one's ever done before, she invited me to stay and have dinner, it's Christmas after all she said, and I was tempted, I was hungry by then but I said I didn't want to intrude and she said I was welcome to join them, she was pretty insistent, now I think back, and I was even more tempted when the smell wafted through, but when I looked inside I saw her husband. I guess that's who he was, in the hallway behind her and the look on his face, what I could see of it, it was dark in there, it said otherwise, he didn't want anyone joining them, and so I said thank you very much but I'd better be going, and I set off back up the path to the valley, or the clough if you prefer, it's up to you.

Looking back, what I did next was the stupidest thing I've ever done, and there's a fair bit of competition for that prize, believe me. I should have just got in the van and gone home, but I didn't want to leave him, the dead guy, up there on his own, not with it getting dark. I didn't like the thought of that, I doubt that he was scared of the dark even when he was alive, being a grown man, but it didn't seem right, him being up there all alone, because those hills can be unfriendly in winter, miles and miles of nothing, which is part of what I like but not everyone does, and I know the cold wouldn't bother him, being dead, but if I'm honest with you, and I might as well be, it wasn't the cold that made me go back, it was the crows. I'd seen a couple of them hopping about near him, and I'm not superstitious, I don't believe that stuff people say about them being bad luck or a sign of death, although this time they'd have a point, but I have seen what crows will do to a lamb if they get a chance, even when it's alive, and I knew I'd never forgive myself if I read in the papers that a body had been found up there with its eyes pecked out, and the papers put that sort of detail in these days if they think it'll make a better story. So despite the cold and being hungry and not having any smokes left to keep me going, I went back up.

The mountain rescue turned up about an hour after me. I could see a trail of torches, or probably headlights, coming round the hillside a little higher up, not the route I'd used, not many people know the routes I use, although maybe the mountain rescue lads do, because they knew exactly where to find him, and one of them, the tall one, he had a flask of tea so I got another free drink, the second of the day, and I needed it too, like I said it gets cold up there in winter, especially after dark when you're not moving about. Anyway, after they'd zipped him in a plastic bag like on TV, one of them, with a big bushy beard, he came over and asked me why I'd come back up, and I didn't tell him about the crows in case he thought I was soft, so I just said it felt like the right thing to do and then he asked me my name, and I hesitated – you can't be too careful – but he seemed like a decent bloke and he wasn't police, so I decided it would be OK, then he put his arm round my shoulder and told me I was a good lad. Now I usually take no notice of what anyone says about me, good or bad, although it's not often good, I'll be honest with you, but I couldn't help feeling a little bit proud because I don't get told I'm a good lad very often, don't deserve to either, but maybe this time I did, so I walked down with them, and bushy beard gave me a coffee, which made it three drinks for the day, and I said goodbye. The tall one and bushy beard waved, so did the one with glasses, but the other one didn't. He never spoke the whole time, which I found a bit odd, but he was busy with the body, kind of took charge of it, so I just headed off.

I didn't think about it for the rest of the week, well that's not quite true, I thought about him, the dead guy, a few times, like I said I'm not superstitious and I didn't know him but it was me who found him and I did wonder why it was me, but after that there wasn't much else to think about, even if I'd wanted to. I went into the hills for a few more walks because the factory was shut until new year and the weather was good, cold but sunny, and those days I didn't see anyone else up there, which made up for my Christmas Day walk being interrupted. I even climbed the Cheviot on New Year's Day, it's not my favourite like I said, but for some reason I fancied it and I'm glad I did because the next day was the first one back at the factory, back to the grind. But before I'd even started my machine up, Trevor, the supervisor, who's alright I suppose, just not really my sort of person, he came over and clapped me on the back and started saying how proud everyone was of me, how I was a hero and it was good publicity for the company, and I didn't know what he was talking about until he showed me a copy of the local paper and there I was, page five – I hadn't noticed the rescue lads taking a photo, I'll be honest, but there I was, name underneath and one of them saying I was a model citizen and it was the perfect story for the season and the world would be a better place if there were more people like me about. I'm not sure I agree, I doubt my family or the police would call me a model citizen, and Trevor wouldn't either, not normally, but today he seemed very pleased with me and said the boss wanted to see me in his office, the one overlooking the factory floor, so up we went and they gave me a coffee, a proper one, not like the machine we've got downstairs, and I was thinking that I'd never had so many free drinks in my life when the boss said there was a reporter from the other local paper, the weekly one, why we have two I don't know, no one reads either one of them, but anyway they wanted to interview me and he was coming down to the factory that afternoon with a photographer. I wasn't all that keen, I'll be honest, because I was already in the paper and I don't like attention. I keep to myself, always have, but most of all I don't want people copying my idea of going up there on Christmas Day, it wouldn't be the same if there were loads of people about, and people would go up there if they thought there'd been a body found up there, people are strange like that, some are anyway, so I didn't say anything and the boss carried on saying it would be good publicity and they could take the photographs next to the company sign in the car park, and there would be a little thank you in my pay. I still wasn't thrilled about the idea, because I'm not the sort who likes attention, it never brings much good, not in my experience, but he was the boss, and a bit of extra cash never hurts does it and it didn't matter whether I agreed or not because he was already calling the reporter back and Trevor said I could stay and finish the coffee and biscuits off, so I decided not to say anything.

The reporter didn't seem interested, only asked two questions, said that was enough which I suppose it was because there's not much more to say is there, I found a body on a hill and some other people carried it down. I didn't want to mention the farmer's wife, if she was a farmer's wife, because I wasn't sure she would want me to, not everyone wants that sort of attention and I don't blame them, I'm the same, and I didn't mention the crows because I'd look soft so I kept that to myself and the reporter seemed keen to get going. The photographer was friendlier, took loads of photos, asked me more questions than the reporter, wanted to know why I was up there, who I went with, where I found the body, whether I'd told anyone about it, but he gave me a fag and I took it even though I don't usually smoke fags but it seemed rude not to so we had a smoke together. Then Trevor said take the rest of the day off, full pay mate, and the boss was over the moon, which is a bit sad when you think about it, getting excited about a photo in the shitty local newspaper no one reads, more adverts than news, but there you go, his choice.

Two days later I was on the front page, there's not much news round here, especially in January, but I was surprised and not entirely happy, no one said anything about the front page and I hadn't done much, just sat with a dead body for an hour, and they were making a big fuss about how brave I was, how society needed people like me, that was a quote from my boss, but I didn't like it. I try to keep my head down these days, life's easier that way. The article was shit as well, just repeating the first one but with a quote from the boss and one from me about how I'd felt cold, which I hadn't even said because saying that makes you look soft and they'd even used the 'Local Hero' headline they use every other issue. But Trevor told me the boss was delighted because it mentioned the factory and the photo showed the company logo, he slipped me fifty quid and I was grateful, of course I was, but I wished he'd been a bit more subtle because the lad who works on the next line over from me was watching so I decided to keep away from him for a while, just in case he asked me about it. He's not to be trusted, none of them are, so whenever anyone asked about the article or what had happened with the boss, I pretended to be busy. I was beginning to wish the whole thing had never happened, or that I'd stayed for dinner with the woman, the farmer's wife, instead of going back up there and to be honest I couldn't wait for the fuss to die down because I don't like being the centre of attention, never have, but no such luck because the boss actually came to my machine himself and said the BBC wanted me to appear on the news later that week, not the proper news, just the local show, but that wasn't the point, I didn't want any more fuss, so straightaway I said no. I'd had enough of it all and he hadn't mentioned another bonus, but he said that was a shame because the company had been having it tough, orders were down, they could use the publicity, and if things didn't pick up then he'd probably have to let a few people go and it would have to be last in, first out, meaning me of course. Then he said someone with my sort of background would find it hard to get another job around here and while I'd normally have told him to fuck off, the fact is that if I don't keep this job I won't be able to keep the flat or the van, and I'd be back to square one which would be a shame because things have picked up a bit over the last year, so I said OK, but as I said it I gave him a look that said I'm only doing this because I don't have a choice and I think you're a wanker for threatening me, and he gave me a smile that said I know that but I'm still your boss, so we both knew where we stood and I felt a bit better for standing up for myself. After he'd gone I told Trevor that the boss said I could have the rest of the day off, even though he hadn't said it, but I knew Trevor wouldn't bother to ask.

I walked on the beach till it was dark, which was quite early being winter, around three, maybe half-past. I told myself after the BBC it would all be over because there wouldn't be anything else to say, and if the boss was as good as his word about the bonus, which wasn't guaranteed, but if he was, then I could get some decent stuff to smoke for a change and everything would soon be back to normal. By the time I got back to the flat I'd decided to go back up to the hills at the weekend, up to the spot where I'd found him, the dead guy, just to get it over and done with, shake off any ghosts, not that I believe in ghosts but better to be sure, just in case, but before I'd even got my shoes off there was a knock on the door. I don't get many visitors so I wondered who it was, maybe the BBC, but I'd had enough for the week. I needed a smoke so I ignored it, but they knocked again. The guy at the door said he was a journalist for a paper in Newcastle and could he do a quick interview, wouldn't take long and there'd be a fee and I wasn't keen, I'd had enough of it all. But then a little extra cash never hurts and the other interview had only taken a few minutes so I'd still have my evening free. He started off with the same questions as the other guy, where I found the body, how I felt, but then he asked whether I'd seen anything lying next to the body, which seemed like an odd question because I couldn't see why their readers would be interested in that, and then he asked if anyone had been up there with me, and who I'd told about going up there, and I was thinking that these were odd questions, and then I realised he wasn't taking any notes and he didn't have a tape machine or a photographer with him, and he hadn't shown me any ID. OK, I hadn't asked him but even so, it didn't feel right, not one bit. One thing people say about me, and they don't say much, nothing much that's good anyway, but they do say I'm a quick thinker and maybe they're right. I didn't panic, didn't lash out, didn't give anything away, just said I had seen something but couldn't remember what it was, hang on, it'll come to me, and do you want a tea mate, I'm having one, and once I was in the kitchen I climbed out through the window, and not for the first time I was grateful that I live on the ground floor and can get into the back yard. With his Newcastle accent, he wasn't from round here and local knowledge was one thing I had over him, maybe the only thing, so I needed to make the most of it and get away, as far as I could, and without any help because I didn't know who I could trust, I'd cashed in any favours I was owed a long time ago, which wasn't many to start with. I ran down the alley between the flats that back onto mine because if he'd brought anyone with him, they'd be out the front, but the problem was I couldn't be sure who he was or what he wanted, all I knew was that it was best to get away from him, because he didn't look like the sort of person it's worth getting to know better. He had a sly face and a smile that wasn't a smile, if you know what I mean, and whatever he wanted to find out from me I didn't want to tell him, and whatever he had planned for me after that I didn't want to be around for, and he would have realised by then that I'd bunked but he wouldn't know where I'd go, so I had to think where he'd expect me to go, which wasn't easy when you don't know the person or what they want, but instinct took me back to the beach. I don't know why but I've always headed there when things weren't at their best, even when I was a kid and dad had come home in one of his moods, it always made me feel better, being near the sea. As soon as I got there I knew I'd made the wrong choice, though, because with the sea on one side there were only half as many directions I could run if I needed to, which I knew by this point I would, sooner or later, so maybe not such a quick thinker after all. I still didn't know who was after me or what they wanted, but I knew it was something to do with that body, and I didn't want to find out what on a cold, empty beach with no one about, so I left as quickly as I could without running, because everyone notices when you're running, especially people who are looking for you and I knew I needed to get to my van.

So now I'm at the van and I'm grateful it's at the end of the street, not right outside the flat. I watch from behind the bins for five, maybe six minutes, doesn't matter, I just need to be sure there's no one near enough to catch me once I make my move, and I can see two men at the other end of the street, and I recognise one of them from somewhere but can't think where, I can't see his face clearly but it's not always about the face is it, it's more to do with his shape and I know he's with the guy from Geordietown and that I need to get away right now. I start the van up, driving slowly at first, no need to attract attention, and only when I'm two streets away do I put my foot down, as fast as it will go, which isn't that fast, my van is a shitheap, but I'm out of town soon enough and there's only one place I'm going, where I've always gone when I want to get away, and soon enough I pull up outside the house of the woman who might be a farmer's wife and where, if I had any sense, I'd have stayed and had a lovely dinner, thank you very much, no one would have known who found him, and as I get out I think what might have been, no papers, no one after me for reasons I don't know about, but there you go, nothing can change that now, and I'm just about to set off into the hills when I realise that's probably the first place they'll look for me, it's one place they know I go to. Thank god the newspapers never mentioned the farmhouse or the woman, because maybe I can hide there for a bit, think about what to do, maybe she'll let me lie low for a couple of days, she seemed like a good sort, so I knock on the door, and for a minute there's no answer, no lights, and I'm wondering what to do when yes, there she is, it's her, the farmer's wife or whoever she is, and she opens the door, lets me in, and I'm grateful when she locks it, no one else can get in, and she says it's alright, sit down and I'll get you a cup of tea or do you want something stronger, and I say tea will be fine thanks, and I sit down and everything that happened with the body and the papers and the Geordie in my flat, it all starts slipping away, finally I'm safe, I've got time to think. I lean back into the chair, look around, it's a nice place, nice kitchen, with a big fireplace and one of those old oak tables, and mugs hanging on hooks on the walls, and pictures of her family, and there's a picture of a man, maybe her husband, the unfriendly one, and paintings of the hills, and I recognise the Cheviot in one of them, and then I recognise my favourite hill, the one I climbed on Christmas Day, I'm not telling you which one, but the one where the body was, then I look again at the man in the picture and I know where I've seen him, he was with the mountain rescue, he was the one who didn't say anything, and he was the one lurking outside my flat tonight, I told you I recognised the shape, it's him, it's definitely him, and I can hear her talking on the phone in the hall.

I know who she's talking to, and I'm mad with myself for not spotting it sooner and for the second time this evening I'm out through a kitchen window and running, running like hell, back up the path, back to the valley, or clough if you prefer, where I found the body and it's not there anymore of course, I saw them carry it down, but it feels like he's still here, lurking in the shadows, laughing at me from the other side, and the one thing I need to do now is avoid joining him and I should go back to the van and drive somewhere else, somewhere they wouldn't think of, but it's too late now because I can hear voices down below, car doors slamming. Sound carries at night, especially when it's clear like tonight and all I can do is run, run and hope they go in the wrong direction or fall over and I get that bit of luck I've rarely had in life, maybe I'm due a bit, I did the right thing after all, going back to wait with the body, everyone said I did a good thing and now I need that karma to kick in but I can't rely on it, I need to keep moving. I know these hills, we've got history together so maybe they'll do right by me now and for a moment I feel better, a little bit safer if not yet safe, and the moon's out, bright, which is another bit of luck because I can see a good distance around me, which helps me keep running, there's nothing else to do, and I don't know which way to go, don't know which way is best, so I head north, away from the Cheviot, because I've never much liked that hill, not as much as the others, I don't know why but one thing I do know is that I need to keep moving, and another thing I know is that if I make it out of this, if I find another body in the hills, then I'm going to leave it for the crows.

6 An Exmoor Carol

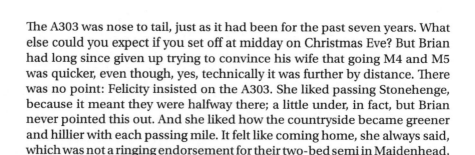

The A303 was nose to tail, just as it had been for the past seven years. What else could you expect if you set off at midday on Christmas Eve? But Brian had long since given up trying to convince his wife that going M4 and M5 was quicker, even though, yes, technically it was further by distance. There was no point: Felicity insisted on the A303. She liked passing Stonehenge, because it meant they were halfway there; a little under, in fact, but Brian never pointed this out. And she liked how the countryside became greener and hillier with each passing mile. It felt like coming home, she always said, which was not a ringing endorsement for their two-bed semi in Maidenhead, but Brian understood the sentiment. He felt the same about going to see his parents. Not that he did very often these days. Felicity didn't get on with them, and that was that.

Feeling a little sleepy, Brian opened his window a fraction. His reward was not a blast of crisp winter air, but the exhaust of a hundred immobile vehicles. *Whence Is That Awful Fragrance Flowing...*

'What are you laughing at?' Felicity asked.

'Nothing.'

'It must have been something.'

'Nothing important.'

Brian didn't tell her because jokes based on Christmas carols were one of the things his wife found annoying about him. Number twelve on a list of seventy-eight she'd prepared for their marriage counsellor. (He had managed two, and those only because he'd felt he had to write something.) To avoid any further questions, he studied the milometer, then the digital clock. They had moved an eighth of a mile in forty minutes. He felt as stationary as those ancient stones in the distance. Radio 4 cheerily informed them that the M4 was moving steadily, but Brian let this pass without comment. It would only cause another argument, and he didn't want to spoil Christmas before it had officially started. Nor did he want anything to disrupt *Carols From King's* on Radio 4, which he'd been looking forward to all journey.

Brian said nothing when his wife turned over to a commercial station playing cheesy Christmas hits by hairy seventies rockers. It wasn't fair, seeing as he was driving, but he decided not to protest. Brian knew he didn't make his wife happy and avoided upsetting her if he could help it. As Slade, Mud and Wizzard blared forth, both of them turned to stare as they crawled past the cause of this latest hold-up: three cars squeezed into the space of one. Drunks, Brian thought. *God Rest Ye, Far Too Merry Gentlemen.* Accidents were almost always caused by men. He could have commented on this too, but his wife didn't need any encouragement to list men's multiple failings, nor to use her husband as a case study for each. So he said nothing. Neither spoke for another hour, until Felicity's phone pinged into life.

'They're already there,' she said, flicking through the messages. 'They went M4, then M5. Gideon says it's much quicker that way.'

'Who'd've thought?'

'Rebekah drove, he says.'

'Is she the one he had the affair with? Or the new one?'

'The new one. And I told you not to mention that.'

'He can't hear us, can he?'

'That's not the point. I don't want anything to upset him.'

Heaven forbid. Nothing and no one were allowed to upset Brian's brother-in-law. Even during the six post-divorce months Gideon had spent living in their spare room, bemoaning loudly and repeatedly his manifold misfortunes, Brian knew better than to point out that sleeping with someone from your wife's tennis club was possibly not the cleverest idea. Especially considering it was the third time he'd done so, to the best of Brian's knowledge. But whatever he said, Gideon would have disagreed and Felicity would have been furious with her husband for causing an argument. So Brian said nothing. He didn't exactly dislike Gideon; they simply had absolutely nothing whatsoever in common. His interests were food, the church choir and cricket, Gideon's were money, hunting and infidelity. There was very little shared ground, and the one person they did have in common had made it clear where her loyalties lay.

Finally they exited the A303, although not before Cliff Richard had cropped up for an unwelcome third time. After passing Taunton, Brian checked the satnav: just twelve miles to go. *Oh Little Town Of Williton, How Still We See Thee Lie.* He always felt his spirits drop at this stage of the journey, signifying as it did that in around twenty minutes the longest week of his year would begin: the week with Felicity's family. He gave a little shudder at the thought of Christmases past, present and yet to come.

Smoke was weaving from the grand old house in the north of Exmoor, signifying the Christmas fire was already ablaze. The lights scattered across the vast front garden were certainly tasteful rather than gaudy. Inside would be equally festive with artfully placed holly and yew branches, and a stack of expensive gifts wrapped in hand-printed paper beneath a huge fir tree. No, the setting was fine. There were far worse places to spend the season.

But there were also far better people. While he was largely indifferent to Gideon, his parents-in-law were much harder to ignore. Geoffrey was loud, rude and pompous, while Emmeline was fussy, vain and pretentious. And Christmas brought out her worst affectations – all "wassailing", "merriment" and "Yuletide" when much more sensible words existed. Even worse, they made little effort to hide their belief that Felicity could, and should, have done substantially better than Brian. And would have done were it not for that unfortunate period with the "wrong crowd" in London, after which she needed someone safe, secure and reliable. Enter Brian: right place, right time and with the distinct advantage of not knowing anyone who sold cocaine. He still wasn't sure exactly how it had happened – she'd turned up crying at his church one Sunday, and eight months later they were married – but he did know he was lucky to have her. Friends repeatedly reminded him of this, and the best man's speech had covered little else. Felicity reminded him too, especially when she was angry, drunk or both. But Brian didn't need reminding. She was beautiful, clever and popular. He wasn't ugly, stupid or unpopular, he was just... well, he wasn't anything much in particular. Nothing compared to her.

His wife embraced her family warmly, the tightest hug reserved for her brother. Brian retrieved their suitcases from the boot, pushing away the uncontrollable dog that was decorating his freshly polished paintwork with its filthy paws. *The Collie Is Too Lively.* As his wife was otherwise occupied, he allowed himself an extended chuckle at this one. After nodding a greeting to his in-laws, Brian took the luggage up to his wife's childhood bedroom. Sitting on the bed for as long as he felt he could get away with, Brian ate half the plate of fruit that adorned the chest of drawers. He'd spotted the remnants of a cheese fondue on the kitchen table, but there was little chance of it being fired up again in his honour. Once again he cursed the fact they had set off late and travelled by the slowest route.

Soon enough, bells rang out for the midnight carol service. On the walk to the village church, Felicity talked with her father and Gideon with his mother. Gideon's partner must have chosen to stay behind, Brian decided, and he hung back a little to enjoy the peal. Felicity and her family walked straight past the homeless man sitting outside the church. Peace and goodwill to all men, except the poor ones. Brian handed him a two-pound coin, wished him a happy Christmas, pondered briefly if that was insensitive, then entered the church. Inside, some well-refreshed worshippers were already murdering the opening carol, sounding more like bagged cats on a riverbank than a heavenly host. *Hark! The Drunken Locals Sing.* When the collection plate came around, Brian kept hold of the ten-pound note he had brought with him, deciding that the man outside needed it just as much as a nameless village in Africa. Charity begins at home, he thought. Even if Exmoor felt nothing like home.

On the first day of Christmas, Brian's true love gave to him gift vouchers. In return he gave her mid-priced jewellery she would never wear. He wondered if either of them would manage to think of something different during the next twelve months, or if either of them would even try. Then, as tradition dictated, he cuddled his wife for three whole minutes, making the most of his annual allocation of affection.

The rest of the day also followed a strict pattern. Champagne and smoked salmon for breakfast, followed by two hours of fireside conversation that didn't involve him, until Emmeline called them through for lunch. As they headed for the dining room table, Brian wondered eagerly what his mother-in-law had prepared this year. For all her multiple failings as a person, he had to admit she was a supremely talented cook.

Quail. They couldn't just eat turkey like normal people, could they? No, it had to be something "gamey" and expensive. As Brian picked through skin and bone in search of flesh, his father-in-law explained loudly that the local farmer only raised fifty birds each year, and just a select few – meaning people like him – had any chance of getting one. Brian helped himself to more minted potatoes to compensate for his disappointing bird, which had evidently been the runt of the brood. The familial conversations booming around the table still didn't require his input, so he turned to Gideon's new partner, who had finally come downstairs after skipping breakfast.

'How's your quail, er...'

'Rebekah. It's fine.'

'What do you do, Rebekah?'

'I work in finance.'

'Really? I'm a fishmonger.'

She smiled thinly, making it clear that absolutely no further details were necessary. This was disappointing. Being a fishmonger – a proper one, with his own shop, and there weren't many of those left now – was the most interesting thing about Brian. If that failed to spark a response, he had nothing better kept back in reserve. Nursing a familiar sense of irrelevance, he ladled another generous serving of braised carrots with green beans onto his plate. He'd done his bit, made the effort. There was nothing more he could do to get to know her. Time to concentrate on his refilled plate, making sure to reserve a little room for the apple strudel and brandy cream he'd spied in the kitchen.

Lunch was always followed by a walk to Hurlstone Point and back. Eight miles, there and back. Or so Felicity told him. Brian never joined them and had never been invited. Not that this upset him: Christmas afternoon was one of the few highlights of his annual visit to Exmoor. Three blissful hours alone to watch the build-up to the Boxing Day Test match while picking through the remains of lunch in peace, the scent of the pine-log fire mingling pleasantly with the tang of the whisky he kept hidden upstairs (Geoffrey had never invited him to sample the household collection). They even took the collie with them, meaning he'd be completely alone. Brian tapped his foot impatiently under the table as he waited for them to leave, using the time to finalise his selection from Emmeline's extensive confectionery display on the sideboard. *Dark mint thins from Marks and Spenc-ahhhh.* His silent thoughts were disrupted by the dining room door swinging open. There stood Rebekah, clad in tight shorts and a luminous pink vest. Brian hadn't even noticed her leaving the table.

'I'm going for a run,' she said briskly to Gideon. 'To Dunkery Beacon.'

'Are you not joining us for our Christmas walk, dear?' asked Emmeline.

'Sorry, strict training schedule. The marathon's only four months away.'

'That's a pity.' His mother-in-law shifted her gaze slightly. 'You're not doing anything, are you Brian. You can let Rebekah back in.'

He nodded, hoping that running to Dunkery Beacon also took three hours and his carefully planned afternoon of TV and grazing would not be disturbed.

'Unless you want to join me?' Rebekah asked.

It took Brian a moment to realise she was talking to him, and his initial instinct was to laugh. He'd never felt any need to see more of Exmoor than the bits that were visible through the windows, and today it looked particularly uninviting. Outside was no snowscape of Dickensian lore, but a medley of low hills beneath a gang of dark clouds that looked like they meant business. *See Amid The Winter Murk.* Those heather moors never assumed the twenty shades of purple depicted in the postcards at the village store, more usually opting for a palette of burnt browns and dull greys. He turned to offer Rebekah an apologetic shrug, but as he did, Brian paused. Her runner's body was outlined clearly beneath skin-tight Lycra, a material which, Brian was almost certain, became see-through when wet. Just at that moment, rain began to hit the windowpane.

'Yes, alright then. Why not?'

To a backdrop of amused smirks and unkind comments, Brian squeezed into an old pair of Gideon's tracksuit bottoms and Geoffrey's discarded tennis shoes. Yet he carried on defiantly and followed Rebekah out of the door, determined to prove his point. Even if he wasn't quite sure what it was.

It only took a few minutes for Brian to realise he had made a terrible misjudgement. Everything he'd always suspected about Exmoor was true. It was cold, wet and windy, and far hillier than he'd ever noticed. He wasn't even able to confirm his theory about wet Lycra, as Rebekah was always too far away. It was only the fear of getting lost, and the further ridicule that would entail, that forced him to go fast enough to keep her in view. The living room, with its log fire, cricket programmes and sumptuous leftovers, had never felt farther away. Up ahead in the drizzle, he spotted her diverting into a barn. He wasn't sure why she needed to take shelter, considering they both must be soaked through, but followed her in a few minutes later, welcoming the chance to see if breath had any intention of returning to his lungs.

Before he had time to find out, Rebekah did something rather unexpected. Facing away from him, she removed her bright pink top to reveal a braless back. It must be a running thing, Brian decided. He had read somewhere that cyclists shave their legs to reduce wind resistance. Even the men, which had perturbed him a little. Perhaps she was wringing out the water for the same reason, or simply to be a little less cold on the way back.

When she turned towards him, though, Brian suspected that something was up.

Rebekah kissed him on the forehead. Their wet faces touched and he wondered what was rain and what was sweat, even if that wasn't the most pressing issue at hand. She kissed him again, pushing him gently towards a stack of hay bales.

'So, er Rebekah, do we go back the same way, or... er...'

His wife's brother's girlfriend tilted her head slightly, regarding him with an unreadable expression. Then she pulled her top back on. 'There's a shorter route back if you're tired.'

Off she went, without so much as looking back. Brian took a moment to enjoy the thought of what had almost just happened, then set off as quickly as he needed to avoid losing sight of her. He even managed to go a little faster on the return leg, a spring most definitely in his step.

Feeling joyful and triumphant, Brian tried to catch Rebekah's eye during the evening meal that Emmeline had prepared (cheeses, port and an array of pickles so staggering that it required four platefuls to sample them all). Rebekah failed to return his glances, which was disappointing, but he noted that she didn't look at, or talk to, anyone else either. Gideon and Geoffrey jousted for conversational supremacy, while his wife and her mother scurried to and from the kitchen. By the time his father-in-law was brandishing the brandy, Brian wondered whether the incident in the barn had actually taken place, or was simply the product of an overactive imagination. Too many pickles can do that to a man.

Boxing Day was consumed completely by another family tradition in which Brian played no role: the hunt. Each year Felicity's family, including that wretched dog, disappeared after breakfast, leaving him cheerfully alone until around four, when he and the other peasants were expected to congregate in the village to cheer the riders home.

Emmeline brought through plates laden with what she described as a "hunter's breakfast", which meant that everything was grilled instead of fried and the eggs were draped with spinach, which Brian found especially objectionable: greenery had no place in an English breakfast, whether cooked for hunters or anyone else. But before he'd even sliced his sausage, Gideon burst into the kitchen, dazzling in blindingly white jodhpurs.

'What happened when you two were running yesterday?'

Brian sighed. He hadn't expected Rebekah to say anything so quickly. Yet she must have calculated, not unreasonably, that the blame would be placed squarely on his flabby shoulders. 'Well, I don't know really, I...'

'She's saying she can't ride because she sprained her ankle, but when I asked her how it happened she said she couldn't remember. Which is ridiculous if it only happened yesterday.'

'Her ankle? I'm not really sure, she was...'

'She's probably worried you won't let her do the marathon,' said Emmeline, placing a soothing hand on the arm of her eldest child. 'You're so caring, always considering what's best for others.'

'You didn't see anything, then?' Gideon demanded of Brian, who was preoccupied trying to think if he knew anyone less caring or considerate.

'No, she was a bit too fast for me.'

'You'll need to look after her today,' said Felicity, barging into the kitchen and looking equally resplendent in her own hunting garb. Brian was indifferent to the fate of the foxes, or the countryfolk whose very existence apparently depended on the sport surviving. But, on balance, he was pleased that hunting hadn't been completely banned. Felicity always looked incredible in that outfit.

'OK, will do,' he agreed, then set about hiding his spinach beneath an extra slice of toast he'd taken solely for that purpose. Soon enough, the hunters set off for the meeting point in the village. *Away In A Ranger*, Brian chortled, although he knew it wasn't his best effort. After making a fresh pot of coffee, he made his way upstairs. It took him a moment to decide whether to knock or not; despite the events of the previous day, or perhaps because of them, he felt an urgent need not to intrude on Rebekah's privacy.

'Come in.'

'Morning. I've, um, brought you some coffee.'

'Thank you.'

'How's the ankle?'

'There's nothing wrong with it. I just didn't want to go hunting.'

'Quite right too. Awful business, those poor little foxes. Although I don't think they're allowed to catch them anymore. Right, I'll be downstairs, shout if you need anything.'

'Stay with me.'

'Really? Well, if you're sure.'

He took the chair in the corner. Rebekah was leaning out of the window, staring at the moor.

'He's having an affair. Gideon.'

'Another one? I mean, I'm sorry to hear that. Is it someone from the tennis club?'

She shook her head. 'Someone he met through work.'

'How did you find out?'

'I heard them talking on the phone. I'm not even sure he's trying to hide it.'

'Well, he's a fool. And I'm sorry.'

'Thank you.' She shuffled to one side, making room for him at the window. When Brian failed to move, Rebekah beckoned him over. The skies were clear and Exmoor looked a little more hospitable than the previous day. Not enough to venture back onto it, but creeping towards picturesque nonetheless.

'So yesterday was...'

'To get back at him? Yes, I suppose so.'

Brian nodded, grateful for confirmation that he hadn't imagined it.

'Today isn't, though,' she said, placing her hand on his.

Brian didn't know what to say. So he said nothing.

'Do you want to have sex with me?'

Brian considered her question carefully, from a number of angles. First he dwelled on how he would explain it to Felicity, should she ever find out. Which she would, as Rebekah would tell Gideon – surely a necessity if she was seeking revenge – and Gideon would waste little time in passing this information on to his beloved sister. Brian could claim it was a moment of passion, a one-off, that he'd lost his head and didn't know what he was doing. Excuses that Felicity used to explain her own indiscretions, which occurred at regular intervals. But Brian wasn't exactly known for his recklessness, so it might not sound convincing coming from him. Plus, he surmised, when you've been thinking through potential excuses in thoughtful silence for over four minutes, you cannot reasonably claim that you were caught up in the heat of the moment.

On the other hand, this was the best chance he was ever likely to have to do something outrageous.

Their first attempt was over rather quickly. Brian got up, feeling a little sheepish, and poured Rebekah a cup of coffee – it seemed only polite – then used her cup to have one himself. It was lukewarm by that point, but still pepped him up a little, and the second time was much livelier. He didn't suggest a third round; twice seemed to be the correct amount. Rebekah got out of bed and returned to staring out of the window. Brian picked up the coffee mug and took it downstairs to rinse. It wouldn't do to let it stain.

The next few days were the most giddily exciting of Brian's life. Each morning he woke up feeling frantic: had Rebekah told Gideon overnight? What would happen when she did?

Would he end up divorced, or would his years of forgiving infidelity be enough for Felicity to extend him the same courtesy? He couldn't stop thinking about all the permutations. Even a flamboyant 139 not out by the England captain in the Test match failed to distract him from the matter at hand.

It was too important, a significant milestone in his life. He was no longer just a fishmonger: he was now a fishmonger who indulged in extramarital affairs. As he picked through a plate of cold cuts, Brian decided he couldn't let this moment pass. His affair with Rebekah was a sign. From now on, he could, should – no, he must – be bolder in every aspect of his life.

It was a cause of huge frustration to Brian that, after such a momentous decision, no one noticed this dramatic shift in his approach to life. Admittedly, the changes were small to begin with – helping himself to snacks without asking, making a cup of tea when he felt like it – but even his bolder attempts failed to raise a stir. He changed over to the cricket highlights halfway through the news, but Felicity and Gideon were so busy arguing about politics that neither complained. At midday on the thirtieth, he went for a drive across the moor, even though it meant missing lunch without permission. No one tried to stop him, and his plate was waiting in the kitchen when he returned. It was all rather disappointing. He had changed, and not insignificantly. But perhaps such acts are only notable when they are made by notable people.

On New Year's Eve Brian briefly considered giving up on his new outlook, given how little impression it had made. But this was a time for resolving to new aspirations, not ditching those barely a week old. He decided to renew his vow to himself. As the family and their partners entered the village pub, he strode confidently to the bar rather than waiting for Gideon to buy the first round as usual. Next, he ordered six whiskies without asking anyone what they wanted. He swallowed his down, then ordered six more, plus a pint of lager for himself.

'You're in a good mood,' his wife remarked, uncertain as to whether she approved or not.

'It's new year, a time to celebrate!' he retorted. She placed a hand gently on his back, the first time she had touched him in almost a week. And she wasn't alone in doing so; the village pub was a safety hazard on New Year's Eve with no room to swing a malnourished kitten, never mind a cat. As more and more people squeezed in Brian and Felicity became separated from the others, finding themselves confined in a tiny spot beside the toilets. After complaining about the smell, the people and the music, Felicity left to find some old schoolfriends who had promised to be there. Brian stood alone, sipping his pint and trying not to catch the eyes of people heading into the gents. He looked over at Rebekah several times. They hadn't shared more than two words since Boxing Day, and she was now busy draping herself over Gideon, oblivious to Brian's glances. He wondered if she had forgiven Gideon, or simply decided to forget about his infidelity for a night, now that she had committed the same sin. Either way, Brian felt let down.

And perhaps a little jealous? He was certainly annoyed, and decided, there and then, that he was no longer the sort of man to give up without a fight. Or at least without a text.

in case i don't make it through the crowd in the next hour happy new year Brian xxx

A few moments later, he checked his phone. The 'message read' ticks had turned blue, but there was no reply. Brian tried again.

let me know if you want to go running some time B xxx

He was reading his message for the fourteenth time, trying to guess what the reply might be (if it ever came) when Felicity barged her way back through the crowd.

'Who's that you're texting?'

Brian wasn't much good at lying. He was too slow to think of anything plausible and too timid to deliver it with anything close to conviction.

'Just Rebekah. I was just wishing her a happy new year.'

'Too lazy to walk over and say it, are you? And you're an hour early.' His wife shot a disapproving stare at Rebekah across the crowded pub, held long enough for as many people as possible to witness. This was it: his moment to confess. When his wife was distracted and might not hear him over the noise.

'I asked if she wants to go running with me.'

'Who?'

'Rebekah.'

'You want to join her running club?'

'Possibly. Or maybe just us. Her and me.'

His wife took a half-step away from him, all that the crowd would allow but sufficient to look her husband up and down. Relief flooded through him, and also a little pride. Finally, there it was: recognition. *Good Christian Man, Rejoice.*

'It'll do you good to lose a few pounds. You've eaten even more than usual this year, don't think I didn't notice all those sneaky visits to the kitchen.Still, rather you than me, I can't stand her. She's so vain, but so dull with it. Can she not talk about anything other than running? It's all training and times and kit and which are the best courses for improving on your personal best. She's so self-obsessed, and...'

Brian stopped listening. He had heard it all before, at least twice a day this past week. He didn't agree, but neither had he challenged his wife on the matter. He would, in time, but not tonight.

'Anyway, I'm going back over to the girls,' said his wife. 'I just thought I'd see how you're doing.'

'That's fine, you enjoy yourself,' Brian replied, noting his wife hadn't actually asked how he was. As she moved away, he checked his messages again. Two blue ticks for the second one as well, but still no reply.

Right, Brian thought. If Rebekah's not interested in me, and my wife isn't either, then I'll find someone who is. With the wild spirit of Exmoor coursing through his veins, he squeezed his way to the bar, next to a woman in a red dress.

'Hello, I'm Brian. Can I buy you a drink?'

There was no response. Brian wondered if he'd done it correctly, not yet being an expert in such matters. He tried again. 'Hi. Let me get this one for you.'

This time the woman turned, frowning at him. 'Aren't you Felicity's husband?'

'Well, yes, as it happens, although...'

'Does she know you approach random women in pubs?'

'Technically just one woman, although...'

But she was gone. Brian felt a little deflated, a little relieved. He wasn't sure what he would have done if she'd said yes. That was the folly of acting impulsively. But when they were back in Maidenhead, things would be different. He would be different. No longer would he be pushed around, or told what to do, or simply ignored. He would meet Rebekah, if she ever replied to his messages. He would visit his parents more often, and if Felicity didn't like it, she could stay at home. Christmases would also be different. Next year, he'd buy his wife something other than jewellery. He would insist on *Carols From King's* on the radio as they drove down. And they would definitely be taking the motorways. *Ding Dong M4 and M5*. Brian laughed out loud at that one, and decided it merited a fresh pint and another whisky.

7 O Brother Where Art Thou?

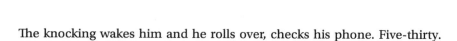

The knocking wakes him and he rolls over, checks his phone. Five-thirty. Uh-uh. No way. He doesn't get up for anyone at five-thirty.

The knocks are slower this time, the rhythm almost sarcastic. Lee gets up to tell his visitor – two words, seven letters – that he doesn't get up for anyone at five-thirty.

It's the Goat. That's different. Lee would do pretty much anything for the Goat.

'We're riding.'

'This early?'

'Best time of day. Roads clear, no pigs.'

'Alright. Gimme five minutes.'

'Three, then I'm off.'

Lee smiles as he pulls on his leathers. The Goat always calls them pigs, like he's in a low-budget gangster film. He smiles again as he recalls how the Goat got his nickname. The Goat tells people it's because he'll eat anything, but Lee's older brother told him the real reason.

It's because he fuckin' stinks.

The Goat's waiting on his bike, engine revving impatiently. A Harley D. 1200T, all sparkling black and silver. Lee eyes it enviously. He'll get a Harley one day, when he can afford one. Biker cliché? Definitely, but as his brother always says, there's no other alternative if you want to be taken seriously.

Yeah, there's faster bikes out there – but who fuckin' looks when you ride past?

'Hey,' says the Goat, interrupting Lee's admiration of his hog. He grabs hold of Lee's chin with one hand, forcing him to look up. 'You heard from your brother?'

'Not since he left,' replies Lee, shaking his head free with a touch of disappointment. He was planning to ask the Goat the same question. As the Goat puts on his helmet, Lee climbs onto his own machine, a second-hand blue Suzuki with too many scratches and half-arsed brakes.

'So, where're we going?'

But his question is unanswered, blotted out by the noise of the Goat roaring down the empty street, trailing a cloud of purple fumes. Lee follows, and a kick of excitement hits when he realises where they're heading. Minutes later he pulls up beside the Goat, screeching to a stop outside the clubhouse – although that description is a little generous. It's a long way from the drinking dens of biker legend, the honky-tonks and dive bars of America's wide open spaces. Instead, it's little more than a lock-up furnished with a noisy fridge and some cracked plastic chairs. The sign above the door doesn't add much to the gang's reputation either. "The South Downs Bikers" lacks the hint of menace that all decent biker gangs should carry. "The Horsham Angels" would have been better, but the playgroup across the road had already snaffled that one. A few people in the town call them the "Wheezy Riders" on account of their leader's obesity-linked respiratory problems, but not when they're out and about. They carry enough menace to avoid that, at least.

Lee exchanges nods and mutters with the assembled crew, people he knows and knows about through his brother. He takes the mockery of his beginner's bike in good humour, even though they all make the same joke. The only person who doesn't comment on his machine is the gigantic specimen now deep in conversation with the Goat.

Danny. The D Man. Big D. Sometimes Fat Dan, but not when he's in earshot. He is the unofficial yet undisputed leader of the South Downs Bikers, and deserving of his status on appearance alone: the thick plaited beard, beer gut and overlapping tattoos are all worthy of the classic biker image. Big D commands respect and fear – isn't fear a part of respect? – from everyone. All except one person, the one who disappeared six weeks ago.

Shortly after his brother had joined the gang, Lee asked if Big D was his hero.

Nah, don't have one. There's no fucker out there better than me.

Big D and the Goat look over and Lee nods back. Nods, but doesn't speak; you don't talk to Big D until Big D talks to you, and he doesn't speak to anyone until he's ridden with them. Which Lee hasn't done, not yet: he was allowed to hang out at the clubhouse when his brother was there, but was never invited to ride with them. Although it looks like today is the day that changes.

'Heard from your brother?' asks Frodo, sitting in one of the chairs. Lee's never learnt his real name, and never felt the need to find out.

'Not a word,' he shrugs.

'While he's missing, we're a man down,' says Jimmy, leaning against his own silver Harley. Jimmy is just Jimmy. Thick, pale and harmless. Like custard, his brother always said, but the nickname never caught on.

'Yeah, I suppose you are,' Lee mutters. He's determined to act cool until they ask him officially. If he's wrong it'll be just another joke, with him once again playing the role of butt.

'Come on then, let's see what you've got,' says Frodo, kicking his bike into life. This is it, Lee thinks. His trial, his chance to join the gang. He knew it would happen one day: his brother, until recently the unofficial second-in-command, promised as much.

Be patient. And when it happens, don't fuckin' let me down.

Lee is thrilled, relieved – and apprehensive. Because at some point in the next few hours, he will have to go through the club's infamous initiation process. Despite being notorious, at least within the boundaries of West Sussex, no one in the town seems to know exactly what it entails: secrecy about the club's traditions is, well, one of its traditions. His brother would never tell him either.

You'll know when you fuckin' need to know.

He wishes his brother was here for his first ride with the gang, but at least the Goat is. He wants to talk to him, to check that he's coming too, but before he has a chance, seven engines rev in unison and roar off through the streets. No doubt waking a few people up, which is half the point. Lee starts his own machine, embarrassed by its meagre little splutter and relieved the others are already too far away to hear.

And the Goat was right: it's the perfect hour to ride. No cars, no pigs, just the occasional lorry to fly past. The orange sun rises into view as they speed along, but his thoughts refuse to shift from his imminent initiation. It must be something dodgy if they need to be out so early, before everyone else is up. And where? He'd like to know that as well. Squeezing every last drop out of his engine, he pulls up alongside the Goat and tries to enquire through gestures. Point forwards, shrug; where are we going? The Goat doesn't respond though, just pulls away effortlessly, leaving Lee marooned at the back once more.

Yet as the outline of the South Downs takes its familiar form ahead, Lee knows. He should have known all along, or at least should have guessed: it's where they always ride, it's even part of their name. His brother has told him the tales that make up another club legend: doing the whole 100 miles in one go, drinking in every pub along the way, illegal rides along the bridleways of the Downs, scattering the sleeping livestock. A thrill rises in him as his bike groans up the Devil's Dyke. A familiar sensation, too – he remembers cycling up here with his brother as a kid, racing each other to the top.

C'mon, hurry up, you little prick.

Lee was desperate to beat him, just once, but as soon as he got close to doing so, his brother swapped pedal power for petrol. Maybe they can have a proper race, when he comes back. He'll return soon enough, Lee is certain of that. But right now he needs to focus: he is losing yet another race up the dyke, struggling to keep pace with the bigger, better machines disappearing over the top. They aren't veering off to chase cows, though, and Lee knows, finally, exactly where they are heading. Of course, he thinks with a smile. Brighton: the city where a hundred thousand bikers have gone before, to race along its seafront and fight beneath its piers. He's seen the films and heard the stories. Most people think those days are gone, confined forever to celluloid, but his brother put him right about that.

This one time, I wrapped a bike chain round the back of some prick's head. Fucker never knew who hit him.

Lee knows that there will be pressure on him from the start to uphold the family reputation. You need a bit of attitude to be a biker, but his swagger to date has been a hand-me-down, assumed rather than proven. Lee knows he can't live off his brother's name for ever. Especially when he's not about. He wonders briefly if he was supposed to bring a weapon, but how could he have known? Anyway, the Goat will have brought something if he needs it. The Goat's always looked out for him, far more than his brother ever did.

Excitement-tinged nausea rises from Lee's gut as they pass the burned-out pier and head east along the coast. Nervously he scans for tooled-up rivals on the beachfront, but all he can see are the dawn joggers and the first round of dog-walkers. No mods, no rockers, no Sting, no Phil Daniels. And his comrades show no sign of stopping, or even slowing down. They are only passing through the city, he realises as they roar past Brighton Marina. Ashamed at his relief, he swallows down the tang of vomit and keeps riding.

But if not Brighton, and not the Downs, then where? Lee scours his mind trying to remember what lies beyond, but his memory is scratchy. Eastbourne is somewhere out there, Beachy Head too, but he doesn't know how far. They never went that far as kids. Briefly, he wonders if he really wants to go through with an unknown initiation in an unknown location, but he cannot turn back. He'd never get the chance to ride with them again, never get the chance to ride with any gang worth joining. Reputations are hard to earn, and even tougher to shake off. Especially in the biker community.

Never refuse a ride, never let your mates down and never back down from a scrap. Do it once and you're fuckin' done. No second chances.

Lee knows he is sealed to whatever fate lies ahead. Steeling himself, he twists the throttle hard and pulls up alongside the Goat once more. Whatever they've got planned, it can't be too bad if the Goat is there. He can rely on the Goat, his brother's best friend since before Lee was born. The Goat was the one who stepped in when playground fights got out of hand, told him which bands to like, gave him his first joint. It was the Goat who'd taken him out on his seventeenth birthday a few months back, pouring a bottle of whisky down him and laughing when he'd thrown it straight back up. Lee knows he'll be fine as long as the Goat's around, and resolves to keep up with him, even if he destroys his bike in the process. It's a shit bike anyway, he needs a new one. Maybe he'll borrow his brother's Harley, if he can find the keys. He still doesn't understand why his brother left it behind. Wherever he is, he can't imagine him there without his Harley.

Abruptly they turn off the main road at a village Lee doesn't recognise. The lane is thin, winding, and can lead nowhere but the sea. By the time he pulls up, the others have already removed their helmets. He sees they are waiting at the top of metal steps that drop over the cliff edge to a deserted pebble beach.

'Down there,' says Frodo, nodding at the steps. Lee turns round briefly, hoping for the Goat's reassurance that it's the right thing to do. But the Goat still has his helmet on, and the visor offers no clues. Unable to prevent them, he's ashamed to feel tears collecting in his eyes.

You cryin' again, you little prick? What's wrong with you, always fuckin' cryin'?

Big D is already on the beach, staring at the sea, by the time Lee gets down. The rest of the gang line up beside him, Jimmy and Frodo standing closest. Only the Goat hangs back, sitting down a little higher up the shingle. The sun is as good as up now, sharing its gentle early warmth with them. Silently, Big D steps forward. He takes off his leather jacket, allowing that vast gut to spill forth. Then he strips. Naked.

Of all the possible initiations Lee imagined over the years, this wasn't one of them. He watches as the mountain of flesh waddles to the water, then realises that the others – all except the Goat – are also naked.

'Get in,' says Jimmy. Lee knows he doesn't have a choice. He strips.

The cold water bites at first, but then invigorates him with a welcome rush of bravado. Each new wave makes his body feels fresh, alive. There are no rival gangs out here, no weapons. Was this all it ever was? Lee begins to feel stupid at letting the musings of local gossips dominate the reality. He sniggers to himself. They aren't even a proper gang, just a group of men who ride bikes and drink supermarket whisky in a lock-up. His brother was a bullshitter, even as a kid, and now Lee sees the full extent of his charade. There are no beach-front fights, no bitter rivalries or high-speed escapes from the pigs. Maybe this is the initiation test: nothing more than naked early-morning swimming. And many, many drinks afterwards, no doubt, once they're back at the clubhouse. Yes, that has to be it; he's been worrying for nothing.

Lee makes himself believe this as Big D drags his walrus-like frame through the surf.

'I wasn't sure if you'd come out for an early ride. Your brother never did.'

Big D has finally spoken to him, meaning Lee can speak back. 'He's a lazy bastard, my brother.'

'Agreed.' The man-mountain ducks under an incoming wave, wiping the salt from his eyes as he rises. 'He's also a thief.'

So that's it, Lee thinks. No wonder he left town; no one would stick around after stealing from Big D. He wants to know what, or how much, his brother took, but this is not the moment to ask.

'Do you know where he is?' Big D asks.

'I don't, honest. If I did, I'd tell you.'

Fuckin' snitch. I always knew you was weak.

Big D looks at him. Stares into his eyes for what seems like an age but is in fact merely the longest half-minute Lee has ever known.

'I believe you. So, next question: are you prepared to stand in for him? Ready to take his place?'

'That's up to you, man. Your gang, your call.'

Big D looks him up and down, making one last check. Then smiles at Lee. 'Yeah, you're ready.'

The leader of the South Downs Bikers exits the water and hauls himself onto the pebbles. The gang's newest member stays in for a few moments more to let the waves break over him, washing the fear from his face and the piss from his leg. He nods at Jimmy and Frodo, standing in the water a few feet away. The he looks over at the Goat, sitting further up the beach, but his brother's best friend is facing the other way. Lee wonders if the Goat knows more about what his brother has done. He'll ask him later, when no one is about.

He ducks under one last time, to cool his mind and the heart that is still beating at twice its normal rate. He listens to the sound of the pebbles moving with each swell, louder than he would have ever imagined.

So loud that he doesn't hear the others move towards him.

Doesn't turn as they grab his shoulders.

Never finds out who holds him under for as long as it takes.

8 Like Father, Like Son

'Where do you fancy tomorrow Ciaran? Pen y Fan?'

'It's gonna rain all weekend.'

'No, the forecast said it'll blow through soon enough.'

'I thought your car was broken?'

'It's fixed now, I told you that. Didn't I?'

'Maybe.'

'That's a plan, then. We'll set off at eight, so we're down before dark.'

'OK.'

The rain didn't blow through. They turned back before Pen y Fan, before Corn Du even. Red kites hovered overhead, but neither spotted them. The boy's lips were blue when they got to Storey Arms car park, only resuming their usual colour after hot chocolate in a polystyrene cup from the van. The boy noticed his father didn't buy anything for himself, but was too cold to ask about it. Back at the flat his father spread the map out to show him the route they would have taken, but the boy fell asleep before he had finished.

'What do you think, shall we try Pen y Fan again? The forecast's much better.'

'Can't we just stay here?'

'Stay in? At the weekend? Come on, Ciaran, look at the map, that's where we got to last time, and we only need to get to there.'

'That's twice as far.'

'No, just under. Come on, the fresh air'll do us both good.'

'I get loads of fresh air.'

'A bit more can't hurt, can it?'

'OK.'

The forecasters redeemed themselves – the sky a brilliant blue, the breeze to their backs. The Usk Valley from Pen y Fan's apex was perfect, the glass-like air revealing nature's full palette: an image to store away for the long days of a working week. The boy wanted to turn back, but his father insisted they push on to Cribyn. All three in one day, that was the real challenge. You'll be able to tell your friends you're a proper mountaineer, he said, but the boy knew his friends wouldn't care. His eyes were half shut at Bwlch Duwynt and fully closed seconds after reaching the hot chocolate van, which had long since shut up for the day. A jay berated them from above, its rasping calls making clear its displeasure at their presence. His father smiled proudly as he sipped on the last of his flask. Like father, like son. That was the plan, anyway.

'Mum wants to talk to you when she picks me up.'

'Talk to me? What about?'

'I was off school for two days the other week. She said it was too long for me. The walk. I got a cold.'

'She doesn't know what she's talking about. Don't worry, Ciaran, I'll sort it out. How's school?'

'Alright.'

'How're the Ospreys doing? It's the Ospreys, isn't it?'

'Yeah. Alright, I suppose.'

'Great. Look, don't worry about your mother, I'll sort that out. Here, this is the walk we're doing tomorrow. Y Mynydd Du via Cwm Tawe. What d'you think?'

'I can't. Mum says I'm not allowed. Not 'till I'm completely better.'

'You look fine to me. Maybe we can do just half of it, get some chips on the way back.'

'OK.'

He thought about his ex-wife while the cat from the flat upstairs made itself at home on the chair. She'd never approved of his walking, and even tried to stop it completely after they were married. You've got responsibilities now she'd told him, and more than once. But shopping and cleaning weren't responsibilities – they were chores, something that could wait until tomorrow. She'd refused to speak to him when he'd returned two days late from a weekend in the Rhinogs, but how was he to know it would snow that heavily? Or that their baby would arrive two weeks early? None of it was his fault. She forbade any walking at all during his first year of fatherhood, meaning he'd missed out on one of the best summers Wales had ever known. The marriage never recovered.

'Sunshine forecast all weekend, Ciaran, how about we take the tent somewhere? I was thinking we could head north a bit, maybe Tywi Forest?'

'I can't. Mum's picking me up early. With Neil. Tomorrow afternoon.'

'Tomorrow? Why not on Sunday?'

'She said you know about it. It was in the letter. From the solicitor.'

'Really? Don't think I've got it yet. Maybe we can do something nearer, get some chips on the way back. I won't forget this time, promise.'

'OK.'

They went to Gower. In the clear light of morning, the father couldn't bear the idea of driving any distance and not climbing a proper hill. But the mist rolled in halfway up Cefn Bryn, thickening to paste before they reached Rhossili Down. They trudged in silence, speaking only when he stopped to show the boy where they were on the map. A hedgehog was spotted outside Port Eynon, but it failed to sustain a conversation all the way back to his flat on the rougher side of Swansea. He'd look for a bigger place soon, where the boy could have his own room when he stayed every second weekend. He'd need more shifts to pay for it, of course. Evenings only, though, not weekends. Weekends were sacred. The boy was asleep before he realised he'd forgotten about the chips again.

'Dad?'

'Alright, Ciaran? What's up, everything OK?'

'Yeah, fine.'

'Your mum OK?'

'Fine. It's about tomorrow...'

'It's up to you, you decide. We can just do a shorter walk so we don't annoy your mum again. What about Glynneath, to see the waterfalls?'

'No, it's... is it alright if I come next weekend instead?'

'What's up?'

'It's Neil. He's got season tickets for the rugby. For the Ospreys. Through his work. He said I can bring a friend.'

'But it's our weekend, Ciaran. Can't you go another time?'

'They only play at home every other Saturday.'

'So is this going to be a regular thing? Changing our weekends?'

'Mum said you got a letter about it. From the solicitor. About the money as well.'

'Can't say I've seen one. Is your mum there? Put her on, I'll speak to her.'

'She's not in at the moment. Can I go, though? To the rugby?'

'OK.'

After his son had hung up, he browsed his maps for a while before settling upon OL13. Two hours later he was pitching his tent in Llanthony, the campsite as busy as ever on a springtime Friday. The next day he completed the Twmpa circuit in three hours, six minutes; not quite his record, but not far off. After a lunch of cheese and pickle sandwiches he set off once more onto Bwlch Isaf, dropping down from the ridge to camp near Grwyne Fawr bothy. On Sunday he returned to Llanthony along the Vale of Ewyas, but went far too quickly. Refusing to drive back early, he nursed a small coffee in Abergavenny. A discarded paper told him that Ospreys had lost heavily to Harlequins; he pulled out his phone. *Sorry about the result hope it was a good game see you next weekend dad.* He shared no news of his own weekend, knowing it would fail to spark much interest. The passion wasn't there – that unshakable thirst for the outdoors, a willingness to do absolutely anything for a day on the hills. He'd nurtured it from an early age, in case it wasn't passed on genetically, but he had failed. It was possible he'd overdone it; maybe three and a half was too young for Yr Wyddfa via the Watkin Path. The Pyg Track would have been a better option, he could see that now. He nearly hit a badger on the drive back, but swerved just in time to their mutual relief.

'Do you want to go to Gower again tomorrow? We could get chips on the way back. I won't forget this time.'

'Can't, I've got homework. There's a test this week.'

'I can ask you questions along the way. What subject is it?'

'Maths. You hate maths.'

'What about Sunday, then?'

'I really need to revise, Dad.'

'OK.'

Instead, Saturday morning was spent tidying up his map shelf, but that took no time at all, as they were never put back out of order. The boy sat quietly, half-reading his maths books. When the rain eased, his father went into the communal garden to remove two dead branches from the apple tree. No one from the other flats would ever get around to it. The boy joined him at eleven-thirty, carrying two mugs of underbrewed tea which they drank together on the bench. The fox sat in its den behind the shed, waiting patiently until it was safe to leave.

His thoughts wandered northwards; some friends from work had gone to the Beacons and he wondered where they'd be. The chip shop was shut at lunchtime – no sign on the door to explain why – so they ate beans on toast and watched game shows on TV. The boy's mum picked him up early, again with no explanation.

'Can we go to walking tomorrow, dad? To the Brecon Beacons?'

'What's brought this on, Ciaran? You've not fancied it since Gower.'

'Nothing, really. I need to get a bit fitter, because... all three in one day, that's the challenge, isn't it?'

'You're on. Chips afterwards?'

'OK.'

An early start was rewarded with a clear run up Corn Du's deeply scoured western path. Only on the main ridge to Pen y Fan did they meet anyone, nodding a greeting as is the walker's custom. The father pointed out the route on the map at regular intervals, eliciting more interest than usual. He pointed out a buzzard, telling the boy of its Welsh name: bwncath, the cat-bird. The boy agreed to do Fan y Big as well, keeping pace on the return leg up until Gwaun Taf. They shared the dregs from the flask at Storey Arms, perched side by side in the car boot. The hot chocolate van had vanished, four piles of bricks left in its wake. As the boy waited in the car, his father rinsed out the lid in a trickle of a stream, unable to remember the last hill day he'd so enjoyed.

'What d'you think Ciaran, Pen y Fan again this weekend?'

'Can we do that longer walk you told me about?'

'Y Mynydd Du? Reckon you're up to it, do you?'

'I think so.'

'I think so too. That's a plan, then. Go and get the map for me. Number twelve.'

'This one?'

'That's the one. Shall we set off tonight, camp nearby?'

'OK.'

They cooked sausages over a gas stove at night, then more for breakfast. The largest of the farm cats enjoyed the fallen scraps once they had left. The boy was ahead for most of the day and, for the first time, beat his father back to the car.

'Ciaran, look here, I want to show you something. What d'you think of that?'

'What is it?'

'That, my boy, is the Offa's Dyke. We're walking it this summer, once school's finished. Two weeks, you and me, right along the border of this fine country of ours. What d'you say?'

'Did mum not talk to you?'

'Talk to me? About what?'

'Rugby. I've joined the Ospreys. Well, the youth team. I've got training all summer.'

'All summer?'

'She said she told you. Neil organised it, he knows someone at the club. He got me in for the trials.'

'Did he now?'

'He said I need to get fitter. And stronger. That's what he said. That's why I wanted to do some walking.'

'So it's all summer, is it? This rugby?'

'Four weeks.' And then it's every weekend when school starts up again.'

'Every weekend? What about our weekends?'

'Mum said it was in the letters. The ones from the solicitor. You have to pay the money, and if you don't, then... and you didn't pay.'

'I meant to do it. I must've forgotten.'

'We can still go walking, if you want. Once it's all sorted out.'

'Yes, of course.'

'On the days when I'm not playing rugby.'

'OK.'

Rugby. Throw and catch for fat lads. He had never understood its appeal, nor its grip on his countrymen and women. Why run around a small patch of grass when you can roam for miles among the mountains? And now his son was afflicted by the national curse, despite his best efforts. The boy turned on the TV while his father stared at the maps he had laid out carefully on the floor. Pins marked the campsites he'd chosen along the route, each fifteen miles apart. The boy's daily limit, carefully observed on their recent walks. He glanced at the stack of letters next to the bed. Their tone had become a little more hostile of late, and the message of the most recent one was clear: visitation rights were to be withdrawn until all backdated maintenance had been paid. The full amount, plus fees. No interest would be charged. Once he had paid, full access would be restored immediately. And if he didn't...

The boy was absorbed, soaking up the rugby results on the TV. There was no hope for him now. A lost cause. Silently, his father began to rearrange the pins on the floor.

He would be much faster on his own, twenty-five miles a day at least. The time he would save would allow for a visit to Snowdonia afterwards. He hadn't been that far for a while. And while the money he had put by wouldn't cover his overdue maintenance payments, it would be more than enough for a few more nights of campsite fees. The mouse that lived behind the cooker watched as the father went to his map shelf to find OL17.

9 Offcomers

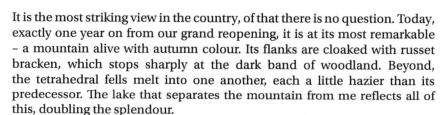

It is the most striking view in the country, of that there is no question. Today, exactly one year on from our grand reopening, it is at its most remarkable – a mountain alive with autumn colour. Its flanks are cloaked with russet bracken, which stops sharply at the dark band of woodland. Beyond, the tetrahedral fells melt into one another, each a little hazier than its predecessor. The lake that separates the mountain from me reflects all of this, doubling the splendour.

The first time I saw it, in February two years ago, I knew I had to have it. Although on that day, I would have happily taken any view on offer – anything to distract me from the interminable board meeting in which I was trapped. I didn't want to be there – not in the meeting, not even in the Lake District – but one of my colleagues, in an unwelcome burst of creative thinking, had insisted that a change of scenery would 'fine-tune our minds' and allow us to 'zoom out to the bigger picture', along with various other corporate phrases that sound perceptive and yet are anything but. The purpose was to agree exactly how many redundancies the company would need to make that year, and our declining prospects were evident in the choice of venue: a run-down hotel set two hundred metres back from the lake. The kind of place that tries to add a touch of glamour by providing cheap sparkling wine with lunch, no doubt trusting its regular clientele won't realise it is nowhere even close to champagne. The whole charade was utterly tiresome and I resented being part of it, especially as I had already informed my fellow executives of my decision to retire. None of the redundancies would be my responsibility, so there was no need for me to be involved. Yet there I was, trapped in an increasingly aggravated discussion about unions, corporate responsibility and two-yearly forecasts.

Rather than contribute – they rarely listened to a woman anyway – I passed the time staring out of the window and across the water. The small thicket of trees on the near shoreline prevented a clear view, yet I was still able to observe how the mood of the mountain opposite changed with each passing hour. Its still-snowy summit accentuated the cold grey-green of its flanks, while the strip of white cloud ravelling down its face accentuated its nuance and depth. Birds glided effortlessly on the hyaline water between us, leaving dissipating arrowheads behind them. As argument and counterargument raged around me, I knew that I had to have this view. To own it. To decide who got to share it and who didn't. I blocked out all else and began to formulate my retirement plan.

At sunrise next morning, I walked down to the lake. I needed to see it again, at its earliest hour, just to be certain. Passing flower beds showing the first shoots of daffodils – such an uninspiring choice – I headed for the bench a little further up the shore. Unobscured by the trees in front of the hotel, the view from here was even finer and the mountain somehow even more spectacular. The sun crept up behind me, illuminating the eastern face inch by inch and painting it with a fresh palette, one of brown and purple and orange, scorched through with thick black shadows cast by its ridges and folds, a shifting show of shadow puppets. The singularity of this view was confirmed by the photographers jockeying for position on the grass around me, some even waiting in line for their turn in the prime spot. Even the joggers paused to take their own mental snapshots.

It is possible to have everything in life and still want more. Once back in London, I could not stop obsessing about the view imprinted so vividly on my mind. During those long final weeks before retirement, I set out the details of my new project: a fully refurbished hotel, five stars and fine dining in place of the shabby old relic where I'd been forced to stay. Something exceptional for those who not only deserve it, but can also afford it. It was just what the region needed: a taste of the top-end, an overdue injection of style and refinement. An alternative to the washed-out places that still, even now, proliferate around here, somehow surviving on two-for-one weekend deals and ten-pound lunches. By contrast, my hotel would be perfect. And the perfect hotel demands the perfect view.

The owner was far too eager to sell, displaying a desperation that rendered his late attempt to increase the price both laughable and pointless. Once the sale had gone through, I appointed the necessary consultants to turn my grand vision into glistening reality. It swiftly became clear that to provide my guests with that exact view, I would need a new building, one closer to the lake, on the spot where those photographers had waited so patiently in turn. The land was now my mine, but building on it would, I knew, be problematic. There was a reason it had remained empty: an awkward tangle of notions such as "access for all", "public goods" and "protected for the next generation". I could understand such sentiments, of course; that spot had snared not just me, but thousands, maybe millions, of others. They all felt their own emotional attachment to that view – and emotion is one of the trickiest hurdles to overcome.

Tricky, but not impossible. Because while emotion pushes people to sign petitions or provide heartfelt polemics on radio phone-ins, it is notoriously difficult to measure precisely. By contrast, jobs, salaries and tax revenues are very easy to quantify, and even simpler to round up to attention-grabbing figures. So before I had even tasked my legal team with drafting the planning application for the new building by the lake, I contacted Bernard, an old acquaintance who had foolishly eschewed the rewards of the business world for the acclaim of academia. He quickly agreed to undertake an economic impact assessment of my new hotel in return for continued corporate sponsorship of one of his myriad research projects. Signing off on this promise of three more years of funding was my final act before leaving the company.

A few weeks later, the learned professor provided a thorough assessment of the many benefits my new hotel would bring, including the welcome boost of high-paying jobs in an economically deprived area. There was also an overview of the type of tourist such a prestigious hotel would attract. Terms such as "high-end" and "upmarket" littered his prose, and the implication was clear: big spenders. The final section of his report was devoted to the "extended regional impact" the project would bring, detailing how the hotel's wealthy guests would also benefit local shops and restaurants. Such prospects are beloved of cash-starved councils, and they are exactly what this place so desperately needs. I struggle to believe that anyone ever planned that the most beautiful corner of England should become overrun with thrifty walkers who stay in campsites and buy a few flapjacks at most. It is unquestionably better for everyone, not least the environment, to have fewer, but wealthier people visiting.

Alas no report, however glowing, can do much to quicken the cogs of democracy. It took nearly five months for planning permission to be approved, thanks to objections to almost everything; grassroots campaigners are nothing if not dogged. First it was the footpath that runs along the shore. As a public right of way, it couldn't be closed. Fine, I said, the new building wouldn't block it, and people could still pass through my grounds as long as they stuck to the path and didn't stray onto what would be my landscaped lakeside lawn. Next, it was those blasted trees which had obscured my gaze on that first day and needed to be removed for the new building. I am certain no one had ever given them a second thought until they were facing the threat of a chainsaw, but once news got out of their imminent demise, every last man, woman and dog suddenly deemed them to be of national significance. For a moment it looked as if the tree huggers would win the day, but my good friend the professor came to the rescue once more. Or, more precisely, his colleague in the environmental studies department whose report concluded that the trees were in no way unique, and an area of woodland twice as large could be planted behind the hotel for a "net environmental benefit". Such phrases reassure local decision-makers, and proved sufficient for them to sign off on the felling. A few weeks later, the university's environmental studies department received a large, anonymous donation, this time from my personal account.

After that, the arguments became more niggly but, thankfully, far less robust. Pensioners who claimed to have been coming here since childhood threatened to chain themselves to the benches, but I knew they never would. The dog walkers and joggers wrote letters to the local paper, moaning bitterly that their morning routines would be disrupted – as if there is nowhere else to go around here! Even the nearby school got involved, with students arguing it was their favourite place to play football, climb trees, catch tadpoles, and various other pastimes the youth of England gave up on years ago. Batting them all away took far more time and money than anticipated, but eventually, as it always does, economics trumped emotion. Councillors could see their tax revenues rising, their unemployment figures dropping, their odds becoming that little bit more favourable in the upcoming elections. An unwritten promise of discounted rates for council events at my new hotel helped to get things over the line.

The next stage was the one to which I was most looking forward. My business career, while enormously successful, offered little space for creativity. This was an opportunity to unleash that potential. I hired the best architects I knew from London and, in terms of renovating the main building, largely left them to it. They know best, that's why they charge so handsomely. My focus was the new building to be constructed near the water. I insisted on a dining hall that faced west, with floor-to-ceiling windows to allow unhindered views across to my incredible mountain. I wasn't interested in how they achieved it, but it had to be just so. That view for diners was to be the hotel's selling point, the justification for the prices people would be paying. I could already picture it: guests rising early to secure a table by the window for breakfast, or lingering long after their evening cocktails, unable to drag themselves away. The architect suggested putting a four-aspect master suite over the dining hall, where guests would be greeted with the sunrise each morning and the sunset every evening. I almost rejected her idea, infuriated that I hadn't thought of it myself. But in the end I agreed. No other suite would have that unrivalled view; I'd be able to charge even more for it. People will happily pay extra for something they know is denied to others.

Too many people dismiss us wealthy as being materialistic. It is a lazy insult, painting us as fools who knows the price of everything and the value of nothing. It is also incorrect: we can appreciate the beauty of the natural world as readily as anyone else. The lower classes have long thought they had an exclusive moral right to enjoy the countryside, ever since they set off on their trespass over Kinder Scout. Yet the key word there is trespass: they were not supposed to be there. Would we have defended it so fiercely if we had not also valued it? No, the wealthy have the right to enjoy England's beauty too. Anyone with money has worked to earn it, or toiled still harder to keep it. We deserve the chance to enjoy what it can buy, and exclusivity is part of enjoyment.

The architects gave way to the builders, who in turn stood aside for the decorators. By this stage, I began using local firms to drum up a little goodwill before opening. Indeed, we were mere weeks away from that momentous day when the news arrived from my legal team: there had been a fresh objection. An elderly foreign couple who lived in one of the houses across the water, near the foot of my mountain, had written to the council to complain that my new glass-fronted building not only ruined their view, but caused an "unacceptable intrusion" due to the reflection of the setting sun each evening. Unbelievably, the courts issued an injunction forbidding any further work until the council made a decision. One option on the table was, incredibly, the relocation of my fabulous new dining hall and master suite to a site further back, adjacent to the main building. To say I was livid would be an understatement; I was tempted to take down one of the antique rifles now fixed to the walls and resolve the matter myself. Thankfully, my solicitor persuaded me to consider alternative solutions.

My informant at the council said there was little room for manoeuvre. Elections were due and no one wanted to be seen siding with a wealthy business owner against a couple of pensioners, a stance that conveniently ignored the fact that I had also recently retired. Adding to my problems was the local paper, which had begun to report that there wouldn't be quite as many, or quite such high-paying, jobs as originally predicted in Bernard's report. This caused quite a stir, and the journalist responsible – an ambitious young man who made little secret of his desire to work for one of the national titles in London – let it be known that he would pounce on any hint of pressure being applied to councillors.

The next suggestion from my legal team was to go after the couple themselves, albeit in a slightly less drastic way than I had first considered. I sent my 'friendly' solicitor around first. As every successful businesswoman knows, it's important to have a nice one and a nasty one, and vital to know when to use each. She explained to the couple that the work was nearly complete, and any delays would, unfortunately, mean a longer wait for those hoping for jobs in the hotel which, in one of the country's poorest regions, would be a significant setback for young people with few alternatives. She came back empty-handed, however, informing me that the couple had little interest in local employment prospects, hailing, as I do, from elsewhere. Offcomers, that's what the locals call us. It means outsiders, those not from round here. And this couple, like so many others who have chosen to make their home here, were concerned with nothing beyond peace and quiet in which to enjoy their expensively acquired corner of the world.

And so it was Professor Bernard to the rescue once more. After I agreed to fund yet another of his pet projects, he swiftly produced a report full of complex diagrams and scientific equations which proved unequivocally that the glare from the windows would trouble the couple for no more than seven minutes a day in the height of summer, and much less in winter, which was a small price to pay when set against the positive economic impact that such an illustrious hotel, one with a unique design that had already been submitted for several architectural prizes – all of them fictitious – would bring to an underprivileged region that, he sombrely concluded, had seen a three per cent rise in unemployment even since the project began.

I was certain that his latest masterpiece would bring an end to the matter, but not one councillor was prepared to put themselves in the firing line. Their solution was a public meeting at which both sides of the argument would be heard, and only after that would they make a decision. Local democracy at its finest. The owner of my chosen decorating firm, who hadn't had so much work in years, informed me that the vote would be close. Many still bore a grudge about their favourite picnic spot being taken away, and those wretched campaigners from up and down the country – the walkers' groups, the conservationists, and those who simply like annoying people with dreams far grander than their own – took the opportunity to regroup and dredge up their own objections once again, in the hope of having the project quashed for good.

You don't reach the top of the business world without learning how to spot ambition in others, though. That young journalist had been a thorn in my side since the start – his first hatchet job had described me as an "embodiment of destructive capitalism" and an "enemy of the Lakes" – but in those words I recognised someone who would write anything to get ahead. I was certain he could be persuaded to switch sides with the promise of a position at a national title, which I was able to offer him after calling in a favour with another long-standing acquaintance. Nothing too sinister was requested; just one or two articles rehashing the oft-echoed problems of retirees moving in and pushing up local property prices, plus a couple more reminding everyone that the hotel would provide an economic boost to the area. Finally, the week before the public meeting, he wrote a short piece about foreigners moving into the area in recent times, citing a couple from Europe who had bought a large lakeside property and were looking to buy up others. A complete fabrication, of course, but sufficient to get the nostrils flaring among Brexit-voting locals. By the day of the meeting, the talk was of little else. And, all of a sudden, British-born outsiders were no longer the focus of their wrath.

I stayed away from the meeting, seeing no need to rile those still opposed to the hotel with my presence. Instead, a few well-prepared locals spoke in my favour: the farmer who was to supply lamb for the new restaurant; the owner of the decorating firm, who talked of the young apprentices he'd been able to hire. Even my new friend the journalist put in a good word about his dealings with me, and how much I cared about this charming corner of England. The vote was closer than I'd have liked, but went in my favour. As I always knew it would.

I hid myself away once more on the day of the opening. The gathered throng – caterers, photographers, television crews, employees, and plenty of fickle locals in search of a free drink – swarmed about the lakeside lawn, a rose garden now in place of daffodils. I escaped to the sanctity of my exquisite master suite and for a while I admired the handiwork on display. The colours that were bold but not dominant, the fittings traditional without being dated, the furnishings confident rather than ostentatious. But nothing could compete with what lay across the water. For over eighteen months, while I'd been busy with legal challenges and contractors and councils, my mountain had been unmoved and uninterested in what was happening over on our side of the lake. Through the windows, it stood as proudly as ever, confident that whatever majesty the human hand created could never compete. I raised a silent toast in its honour before heading outside to fulfil my various roles as humble proprietor, visionary entrepreneur and leading local employer.

The evening could not have gone better. Graced with stupendous late-autumn weather, people ate and drank until early morn. A smattering of hand-picked local celebrities gave the event a dash of glamour – writers, painters, poets, certainly no TV stars or footballers – and even the rural plebeians seemed to acknowledge that they were witnessing the start of something significant. The next day my favourite local hack produced a glowing four-page colour spread, packed with gushing quotes and excessive adjectives, plus a gallery of splendid images which all – at my insistence – included my mountain in the background. Tucked away in the latter pages of the paper that day was a tribute from his colleagues, thanking him for his years of service and offering their best wishes for his new career in London. I allowed him to enjoy it for three months before making the call to my friend, his new boss: enough time for him to be tied to a crippling rental contract that he could never hope to cover once he had been fired. A harsh lesson, and a totally avoidable one if only he'd apologised for insulting me in his early articles.

And so, after considerable effort and greater expense than I'd ever envisaged, my hotel was open for business. I bought a four-bedroom place for myself just beyond the national park boundary, where prices are slightly less ridiculous. With a manager for the hotel appointed – poached from my favourite resort in the Swiss Alps after I convinced him he needed a new challenge – I sat back to watch my grand scheme blossom and, finally, the money to start flowing inwards instead of out.

The complaints began even before our first month was through. The dining hall had no privacy, said the guests, as the huge windows meant that people passing by could watch them eat. Others said it was too cold in there. Which was nonsense, of course, and I even installed an antique thermometer to assuage their doubts. But a landscape of frost-capped fells can, it seems, make people feel cold, even in the confines of a fully insulated and expensively heated building. And people are so very eager to share imagined discomforts in lieu of any actual ones. Even those who didn't complain failed to appreciate what they were experiencing, with eyes more commonly fixed on their phones, their food, or occasionally their companions. Anywhere other than my mountain.

They also failed to appreciate the master suite. Complaints ranged from the noise of the diners below to the smells from the kitchen, and again the imagined cold. Yet as autumn changed to winter, by far the commonest cause for complaint on those insufferable online review websites was the dining hall windows, my Italian-made, nine-foot-high windows. There's too much sunlight; the rain is too loud; why are there no blinds to stop people looking in... The unique opportunity to admire the finest view in the land was never remarked upon. Not once.

The final straw came during that first winter. Bookings were below half-occupancy and I had already been forced to lower prices after less than four months of operating. As I passed through the reception on my way to meet, and possibly sack, my manager, I heard someone complaining. He was rich, arrogant and trying to impress a woman who was clearly only with him for weekends away in expensive country hotels. But the nature of his grievance hit me like a fist: he didn't like the view. For three hundred and fifty pounds, he expected more than just a lake and a mountain. The girl on reception tried to placate him, but I cut her off before she had even completed her sentence. Give them a full refund as long as they leave immediately. I won't let anyone talk about my mountain like that, especially not in my own hotel.

It was clear to me by then that somehow, somewhere along the way, I had got it wrong. My vision was wasted on other people, whether rich or poor. I summoned my team of architects once more and explained what needed to be done. And so, after five months of further renovations – if that is indeed the word for making something less fantastic – it went back to what it was: a low-budget hotel. Cheap and cheerful, affordable to anyone and, since opening for a second time, almost fully booked. The rooms in the old building were stripped of their carefully curated flourishes and made available at a third of the price, while the state-of-the-art conference room now holds little more than tables, chairs and a second-hand coffee machine. The facilities that leading companies demand were all removed, because the leading companies never came to use them. The new dining room, built quickly and cheaply over half of the car park, now serves foreign lager and unremarkable burgers to people who like to be sated with change from a twenty-pound note. I even installed a log fire so no one will ever again complain of feeling cold. A fake one, of course. You can't expect real logs at the prices I now charge.

The trees I felled and promised to replace have finally taken root, although rather than doing so in a nearby field, they now form a neat row between the old hotel buildings and the sparkling new construction near the water. The latter is now my residence, and quite possibly the most expensive private home in the country. The master suite is my bedroom, and the dining hall – my brilliant, beautiful dining hall – is the office from which I now manage the hotel myself, ensuring it matches the tastes of the lower classes. Once grown, those trees will become a barrier, affording me a little privacy from the riff-raff who now comprise my clientele. More importantly, they will block off all views across the water for anyone except me. Never again will my guests be confronted by a mountain too grand for them to behold, or be disturbed by a majesty they cannot appreciate. That burden is now mine, and one I bear alone.

Well, almost alone. The lakeside walkway is, unfortunately, still open to the public, and new paths keep appearing as people criss-cross my land to their preferred spots. According to a dog walker who insists on making conversation as I take my morning coffee by the lake, these are known as 'desire paths'. I, however, refer to them as evidence of illegal trespass in my letters to the council. It's costing what little is left of my fortune to have these wanderings legally curtailed for good, but it's worth it. Mountains may be for all, but views of them should not be. And the finest ones should be reserved for those of us who are willing to pay the price.

10 Oology

Egging.

It's a word associated with a bygone age, one little used today. You might chance upon it in an old children's story - something by Enid Blyton, perhaps, or Richmal Crompton. But it is seldom heard in everyday conversation, unless in reference to some attention-hungry idiot attacking a politician. The term, in its original sense, has become antiquated. Yet it is not fully obsolete: the practice persists as the pastime of choice for a very small, very secretive set of individuals. Oh yes, egging - or oology, if you prefer the scientific term - definitely still takes place. But it does so in the shadows, hidden from society's disapproving, easily distracted gaze. It is a secret protected with a fierce commitment that is utterly central to its clandestine continuation.

While not a collector myself, I can understand the fascination the practice has for its reclusive circle of devotees. Jeremy, for example, has been scanning the hidden corners of the Cairngorms for nearly two years now, desperate to add an osprey egg to his collection. And understandably so: they are beautiful specimens, a light pinky-white shell dappled with chocolate-coloured spots towards its base. The birds are not especially rare, but it takes considerable time to locate a suitable nest. Indeed, the pursuit is most certainly part of the thrill for collectors, requiring that mix of enthusiasm and dedication that all fanatics possess, whatever their chosen field of interest. Do not underestimate their knowledge either, for hours of study and observation must be dedicated to their cause. Then, of course, not all nests are viable - a pair may fail to mate successfully, for instance - and the hunter can only determine if eggs are present through hours of careful watching. Even among those pairs that do lay, the oologist must locate a nest that is unknown to, or at least unobserved by, any local rangers or amateur ornithologists.

The knowledge required extends beyond the where: the when is also pivotal to the art. Now, the common man or woman, regardless of how stupid they are, will surmise that egg collecting must take place during the breeding season. But how many know that this can vary greatly, even within a species? Osprey pairs within the same region can lay up to eight weeks apart, so the collector's observations must begin long before the breeding season commences. Furthermore, he – and it is always a he – must select the exact moment to strike, ideally when both parents are off the nest and there is no one about. With all these factors to consider, the window of opportunity might be exceptionally brief, and he needs to be ready the second it opens.

Jeremy's dedication has paid off. Today, we are completely alone and the female, who was keeping guard, has just flown off. This place, specifically this nest, is known to no others, hidden deep in a forgotten glen that has a rich, earthy aroma of decay, the signature fragrance of a place where the sun rarely reaches. More significantly, it is far from the footpaths that criss-cross the mountains and glens, and the nearest road is several hours' walk away. We are a long way from the cafes and outdoor shops of Aviemore, or the underused skiing infrastructure that scars the central massif. There is virtually no risk of us being spotted by accident. No guided groups venture out here, and certainly no picnicking families. There are no RSPB wardens about and certainly no *Springwatch* cameras, although I do believe that the male is a descendant of one of the celebrated Abernethy birds who shot to televisual fame on that programme. It would be the right age, yet I cannot be certain having not spent as long observing the pair as Jeremy. He has spent every weekend up here since winter, choosing his targets with considerable care and observing their progress meticulously. It is three years since the male flew his parents' nest, both literally and figuratively, and this glen is within the standard distance from there. What I do know for certain is that this is his second attempt at breeding. No one wanted him last year, the poor old thing.

One fact of which I am sure is that today is Jeremy's first attempt on the nest. This is the point at which another of the key skills within the egg collector's repertoire comes into play: courage. While some birds build nests that are easily raided, ospreys locate theirs in the most inaccessible spots, high up in treetops or perched on cliff faces. They really are the most inconsiderate creatures in that regard. As a consequence, the collector often needs advanced climbing skills to reach whichever vantage point the birds have selected. And he must ascend alone, with no backup in place should things go wrong. This is a hobby for soloists, and one not without its risks. A few, of course, have even lost their lives in pursuit of their treasures. The last to succumb was Colin, a few years ago now. Yes, courage is most definitely required. This pair have selected a smallish Scots Pine growing halfway up a crag in the danker end of the glen, and I watch as Jeremy begins to test his resolve, and indeed his agility.

He has little need to worry with regard to the latter, however. Over the past few months of following his ventures, I have observed that Jeremy is an exceptional climber, and today, in anticipation of an opportunity, he has brought all the necessary equipment with him: ropes and carabiners, thick gloves to protect himself should the birds return before he is down, and of course a soft-lined bag in which to safely transport the precious eggs. He spends a few more minutes assessing the climb, and is right to do so. The nest is perhaps fifteen metres above ground, and the tree is immature, spindly towards the crown. It is bound to sway a little as he ascends.

Satisfied, he takes one last look around to check there is no one about. This, by contrast, is unnecessary. Most of the idiots who comprise the Great British public could walk right past us and not recognise what is taking place here. Few noticed the retreat of egging from newspaper columns where reports of arrests and seized collections were once something of a regular feature, and today most citizens are wilfully oblivious to the remnants of the practice. This is partly due to the collectors themselves, of course, who, once again displaying their assured judgement, decided it was preferable to slip quietly into the margins. There were no alliances formed to defend their right to continue this ancient hobby; no marches through the streets of London to counter those trying to stop them. Public outrage can quickly lead to your way of life being condemned, possibly even banned. It's far more prudent to stay quiet, keep your head down and trust the fickle British public to be swiftly distracted by the next worthy cause.

That's where the fox hunters got it wrong, you see. They made a show and quickly found themselves on the wrong side of popular opinion. They pitched it as 'us against them' but misjudged the mood – easily done, given the apathy that generally pervades in our country – and, albeit by a small margin at first, found themselves losing the argument. When given a choice between foxes being violently killed or not being violently killed, the average person in the street will opt for the latter, if you can distract them from their screens for long enough to offer an opinion. We are, after all, a nation of self-appointed nature lovers. We simply cannot abide cruelty to animals.

Except pigs, of course. And cows. Not to mention the chickens guzzled down in their daily fried millions. But the others – anything, in fact, that doesn't fit snugly in a takeaway box – are cherished as beasts worth fighting for. Until they damage our gardens, of course. Snails, slugs, moles, even aphids; they also fail to make it onto the list of creatures we care so very passionately about. Mice and rats, too. They're vermin: they don't count. As are any seagulls that dare to seek nourishment for their chicks and, indeed, any bird that dares to defecate in a place where we might want to sit or stand or park our cars. We are happy to treat with the utmost contempt any creature which inconveniences us slightly.

At least until a self-appointed guardian of the natural world takes up its cause and rallies the online pitchfork-wielders into action. It's bees at this particular moment. They're declining, which means there's online trouble afoot for those evil pesticide manufacturers. Bees are popular, you see. People like them. Wasps, by contrast, people would happily see the back of. The margins are exceptionally fine: one set of yellow-and-black stripes will get you an online petition, another will get you a rolled-up newspaper.

On reflection, it's unsurprising that people are so confused. How is the common man or woman supposed to know what to think when the messages are so contradictory? Take our beloved heirs to the throne, who campaign passionately to end the slaughter of Africa's wildlife before jetting off to their country estates to blast the life out of Britain's less photogenic species. Or the shepherds, those noble stewards and stewardesses of our countryside, whose numerous books and social media accounts overflow with images of their honest, salt-of-the-earth toil as they tend to their flock. There are, you will quickly notice, far fewer pictures from the abattoirs in which the beasts end their days. No, that would ruin the myth. It would be exceptionally bad for their profile.

And profile is important. The public are lazy, stupid and easily led – it only requires a populist cheerleader to point them in his or her approved direction, then sit back and watch as the Twitter witch-hunt gathers pace. If they are a celebrity of sufficient importance, before long their supporters will be shouting incoherently at each other online oblivious to whether anyone on the opposite side is even listening. Take the shooting industry. They are currently under the online cosh, as millions show their righteous fury by tapping on their phone: the perfect form of activism for those who want to make the world a better place without having to leave the sofa. But the shooters don't appear to be too concerned, carrying on as ever they did. They know they just need to be patient, to wait out the storm: attention will shift elsewhere before long. Perhaps back onto the fox hunters, or maybe the extensive and ever-expanding chicken-slaughtering industry. It all depends what our celebrity environmental cheerleaders decide is the next urgent cause. But wherever the public ire is pointed next, it's safe to say it won't be on the egg collectors. There are people who will make sure of that. Especially at the BBC.

He was one too, you know. Packham. Stole a kestrel chick as a teenager and reared it. It's all in his book; you can read it for yourself. A book that received rave reviews from almost all sides, without so much as a hint of condemnation. It was fine for him, you see, because he is fascinated by nature. Attenborough, too; he collected all manner of creatures as a boy, and even sold live newts to his father's university. Does he get vilified? Of course not; he's our best-loved naturalist, a modern-day saint, not some petty vandal wreaking havoc on his local wildlife. It's a tradition that goes all the way back to Darwin. If you profess a love for the creature whose life you are ending, then it's perfectly acceptable. You might even get a phenomenally well-paid TV career out of it. And when it comes to directing the national ire towards your current foes, all you have to do is write the tweet. It takes but a second, and little longer for your millions of followers to click the 'like' button or, if they're feeling truly outraged, retweet it. Given the short attention span of the public, it's perhaps surprising that the egg collectors haven't suffered their own brief spell in the online dock. But no one is interested in them, or what they get up to.

No one except me. I follow their activities exceptionally closely. And Jeremy is the current object of my tenacious attention. I've had him in my sights for several weeks now. Metaphorically at first, and now literally.

Two pellets lodge deeply in his right thigh. Even from this distance, I can hear that distinctive sound as they pierce material and then nestle into flesh. He howls, and there is a crash of branches as he descends far more rapidly than he is likely to have anticipated. Staggering up quickly, he clutches the fresh wound on his leg and inspects the damage. Fear briefly gives way to anger and, as with the others before him, he scans the horizon urgently to see who shot him. There's no danger of me being spotted, of course. I'm far too well hidden for that, and have sufficient supplies to remain in place for several hours, should the need arise. But they never come looking. Who goes in search of an unknown enemy with a gun? Once the shock subsides, they realise they must get away. So it is today as, after another quick glance around the glen, Jeremy begins to limp through the trees that separate him from me. I allow myself a satisfied smile. He has a very long walk out on one leg. He'll probably make it, but it will be slow and painful and his wound will be an infected mess by the time he reaches a road. He won't be out collecting again for a very long time, possibly not ever if the damage to his leg is sufficient.

And there will be no repercussions for me. Who would he report it to, even if he knew who did it? The police? No, the egg collector's innate need for anonymity overrides all other concerns; the desire for secrecy trumps that for retribution. He is unlikely even to admit what happened to any other collectors. They tend not to socialise; as I said, this is a hobby for those whose natural state is alone. Which suits me just perfectly, as it means my victims do not inform the others of their misfortune, keeping those still active sufficiently off guard. To the best of my knowledge, there are fifty-seven collectors in the United Kingdom and Jeremy is my sixth successful hunt. Fifty-one to go to complete my own perfect collection.

It didn't have to be this way. I am certain that, as with fox hunting, most people would agree that egging should be stopped. But for someone to agree with you, they must first be paying attention. And so very few of them did. No one wanted to sign my petition or join my mailing list. For whatever reason, egg collecting failed to strike the necessary chord. My website listed the names of the collectors, but no one ever visited. I wrote weekly letters to my MP, but she never replied. I set up a Twitter account, but no one followed me. Not one of our famous tree-hugging celebrities would support me, despite repeated requests for their help. They never wrote for my blog, they never showed up to my events; they wouldn't even like my tweets. They won't do anything unless there is something in it for them. That proud British tradition of "How can I help you?" has been shunted aside, making way for "How will this help me?". All I needed was a brief loan of their profile, but even that was too much to ask.

And, ultimately, profile is what I lack: the celebrity status that guarantees people will hang on your every word, whatever it happens to be that week. If you are famous, the idiots will follow you on Twitter, Facebook, Instagram or wherever else you have a 'presence'. If you are really famous, a few will even join you on marches through London – always London – on a summer weekend, wielding barely legible signs demanding action on the latest selection from your pick 'n' mix environmentalisms, whether it be ocean plastics, grouse shooting, pesticides, food waste, factory farming, zoos, oil pipelines, Faroese whalers, burning rainforests, fur coats, air miles, SUVs, fracking, Chinese medicine, dog breeding, veal, ortolans, climate change, monocultures, food miles, dam construction, ancient woodlands, or any one of a million other noble causes. And have these marches and online petitions brought an end to anything? Have they stopped climate change? Or hunting? Or cruelty to animals? No, they have not.

But I am stopping the egg collectors. One by one, I am picking them off.

11 Pegs

I've never liked them, not since I was a kid. Don't get me wrong, I'm not one of those 'I don't walk through your garden' types. The countryside's for everyone, I understand that, I'm a reasonable man. People are allowed to use the footpaths crossing our land. They're welcome to, they have that right. But stay on the bloody footpaths! That's all I'm asking. It's like my dad always said, rights come with responsibilities, and it's them that don't keep to their end of the bargain I can't stand. The ones that climb over walls and fences, leave their rubbish everywhere, let their dogs run wild despite all the bloody signs telling them not to.

'That one? Thirty pound. What? So don't buy it then, no one's forcing you, are they?'

Where was I? My dad, he never liked walkers. Farming's a hard enough life, we don't need the extra work, that's what he always said and I agree with him. How could I not? Saw it with my own eyes, didn't I? There was this one time, it was my birthday – seven or eight, I can't remember which – and we were all sat down for my birthday tea, with cake, ham sandwiches, jelly, all of that, but the best thing was that my dad was with us for once, looking knackered, of course, but still there. Well, we'd hardly got ourselves started when the phone rang, and dad had his jacket back on before he'd even finished speaking. Didn't get back until two, and all because some idiots had left a gate open and our sheep were out all over the place. It's not hard, is it? Just shut the bloody gate after yourselves.

I was proper angry after that, I can promise you. So the next day, I went and hammered a bunch of rusty nails into the stiles and fences in the farmyard, hoping to snare one of them bloody walkers. For weeks I sat and watched them setting off, all lugging massive packs about like bloody donkeys, hoping to see one tear a jacket or cut a leg. But no, nothing, not even a scratch. Maybe I just didn't see it happen, most of them go north from here, up over Kinder and onwards. Anyway, I had to remove them all when my mum found out, she was proper fuming. Dad didn't say anything, but he gave me a quid when I'd taken them all out. He'd have done the same himself, I reckon. Not that he'd ever have had the time

It's not his worry any more, mind. He had to retire early, only just past fifty, which meant I took over at twenty-six. I'm not saying that walkers caused all his heart problems – his forty-a-day habit was the main thing, I'll admit that much – but they didn't help, that's all I'm saying. All those extra hours clearing up after them, lambs lost to dogs, always repairing walls and stiles and fences. The weather does enough bloody damage, it doesn't need any help. It took a good few years off the end of his life, I'm certain of it. So when, after he'd passed on, God bless him, my wife decorated the spare rooms to do bed 'n' breakfast, well... he wouldn't've liked that, strangers in the house. Mum neither, God rest her soul and all.

I don't like it myself, but it makes sense, I'll give her that. Financially, I mean. It's a big enough house and you can't make a living from farming these days, you have to branch out a bit. And with the farm being so near to Kinder, well, we get a lot of people passing through, as you can imagine. I saw them as a bloody nuisance; she saw them as a way to make a bit extra. Besides, she was keen for something to do, something by herself. She's not from a farming family, see, and didn't want to get involved in that side of things. Can't say I blame her. She seems to enjoy it, too, despite all that extra cooking and washing.

Me, I can't stand them, round my bloody breakfast table, moaning and complaining all the time. How many ways are there to fry a bloody egg? Butter, pan, done. Salt if you want it, that's up to you. But to hear the way they speak to her - too hard, too soft, too much butter, try using olive oil – well, I'd've turfed them out without a moment's thought, if she hadn't told me not to. One of them, he even complained that his eggs were too small. Take it up with the chickens, man, don't have a go at my wife.

'Sleeping bags? What sort are you looking for? Eh? What do you think I mean? How big, how warm, what colour. Well if you don't know, how am I supposed to? Go and have a look on the back shelf.'

Bloody idiot.

House guests are one thing, mind, but it's the campsite I really can't stomach. When my wife suggested we turn the bottom field, the one by the river, into a campsite... well, all I'm saying is I'm glad my dad never got to hear that. His best field all covered with tents? His heart would've stopped on the spot, fags or no fags. No, it's for the best that he wasn't around to see it happen. That was a damn good field, perfect for overwintering, and now it's full of tents. Not in winter, not so many anyway, but the campers churn it up that bloody much in the summer it's of no use to man nor beast once they've buggered off for the year. OK, they bring in a bit more money, I'll admit that, but that field is where we kept our best ewes for years, decades even. That field had *history*.

It was too much for me at first. Couldn't accept it. I blocked up the ditches one year, tried to make it too wet for camping. Didn't make any bloody difference, though, did it? They all just slept in the mud, we had more of them than ever that year, would you believe? The bottom corner, right by the river, it's a quagmire come spring, but people still pitch down there. We even won an award for the best campsite in the Peaks. It'd be funny if it wasn't so bloody tragic. I've won nothing for my ewes since they were evicted from their favourite patch, mind. Not surprising, is it?

It was late May, two years after she opened the campsite, when I proper snapped. It was pissing down with rain, with a big storm forecast, so I was out checking everything was tied down, that it wouldn't blow away. Gone seven it was, and just as I was allowing myself to think about getting inside for the night, I spotted them traipsing through the yard. I watched from over the wall, just to see if the last one would shut the gate. Course she didn't; I knew from the moment I saw them they would leave it open. Schoolkids, they were. Anyway, I went over and started telling them about shutting gates, even pointed out the sign to them. And their teacher, he starts having a go at me for shouting at kids! Unbelievable. OK, maybe I did use one or two words I shouldn't, not with kids about, but really, who's at fault here? Who's going to tell them what they should and shouldn't be doing in the countryside? He wasn't bloody going to, that much was clear. I had to stop myself clocking him one, I was that mad.

Fifteen minutes later, I've finally got a brew in hand, and there's a knock at the door. Guess who: only that bloody teacher asking if there's any space in the field, even though they haven't booked, because they don't want to go any further. He even says they'll shut all the gates after them this time, laughing he was, can you believe it? I'm about to tell him where he can stick his bloody tent poles when my wife comes through and says yes, of course they can camp, and gives him one of the little laminated maps she's had made up of where everything is, then the little tags to put on the tent to show they've paid. And at that point he says he hasn't got any money and can we email an invoice to the school? So my wife says course we can, not a problem, big smile. Well, I had to take myself upstairs at that point. I was madder with her than him, truth be told. Still, the next half hour was the best I'd had in months. Years, maybe...

The storm had started kicking up proper and, from the armchair, the one by the bedroom window, mug of tea in hand, I watched them trying to get their tents up in the wind and rain and mud. Bloody clueless they were, putting the inners up first so they were soaked before they'd even worked out which bit went over which. They got the poles all tangled up and this one poor kid, who looked like he was having the worst bloody day of his life, he left his sleeping bag and clothes out while they put up the tents. Soaked they were, by the time they'd finished. It gave me a smile at the end of a hard day, I don't mind admitting. A bit of karma for leaving my bloody gate open.

'Gas cans? Two pound or three, depends which type you need. How should I know, I've not seen your stove, have I?'

Honestly, some people. Shouldn't be allowed near naked flames, that sort.

Hang on, what was I saying? Oh yes, those schoolkids. Anyway, I woke up at three, there was a door swinging in the wind and it's a funny thing, but even though you could hardly hear it over the wind, I knew exactly which one it was. The left one on the old barn near the start of the track up Kinder. I grew up on this farm, know it better than anyone now my dad's gone. Maybe it's all farmers that can do it, tell a barn door just by its squeak. Dad could do the same. I'm not saying it's anything to be proud of, it is what it is. Anyway, the quickest way down there is through the bottom field, the campsite, and as I was walking through the field, I stopped. Even though I'd had a good laugh at them, I was still mad. Not with the kids, not so much; no, it was that teacher. Making jokes, mocking me outside my own bloody front door. If he'd said sorry first, then fair enough, bygones can be bygones, I suppose. But he didn't, he just stood there, asking for a favour not fifteen minutes after having a pop at me. Two favours if you think about it. So I decided, there and then, to get my own back. To make him pay. Something small, just to settle the score. So I took two pegs from his tent. Nothing major, but it made me feel better. An eye for an eye, a peg for being a cheeky bastard. I put them on a shelf in the barn, the one at the back, then tied up the door. Didn't think any more about it.

Next morning was a stunner, they always are after a storm. I'd finished my mid-morning brew and decided it was as good a day as any to fix the barn door properly, no point leaving a thing like that to get worse. And who did I find in the field? My old friend the teacher. Normally the campers are off early, but there he was, on his hands and knees, crawling through the mud and looking for his missing pegs. He even had those kids looking, the miserable old bugger. I could've told him where they were, and might've done if he'd so much as looked up and said good morning. But he didn't, did he? Course he didn't. So, when I got to the barn, I stood them up on a shelf at the back, sort of like a tribute to dad, a trophy taken from the sort who caused him so much strife over the years.

After that, it became a bit of a tradition, a ritual if you like. Any campers that were rude, or turned up late, or without booking, or were making noise, or leaving rubbish about – anyone who got my nerves, you could say – I took two pegs from them. I'd make a note of their tent, then sneak out in the night and punish them. The wife never noticed, she sleeps right through, running a B&B is more tiring than you'd think. And the morning after I'd find any excuse to pass by, to see what they were doing. Most of them didn't notice, of course, it's just a couple of pegs, but a few would be there like that bloody teacher, hands and knees, searching for pegs that weren't there. I always enjoyed that. You waste my time, I'll waste yours. Dad would've been proud, he would've given me more than a pound. Each pair of pegs added to the shrine were a nod to his memory and a little bit of recompense for what those bloody tents have done to his best field.

Now, didn't I tell you I'm a reasonable man? That I respect people's right to be here? Stick to the rules and you'll get no trouble from me. One day, must've been last April, maybe May, I saw someone coming down off Kinder. His dog was on a lead, he shut each gate, then soon enough, he was knocking at the door, asking about the camping field. He apologised that he hadn't booked ahead, pleases and thank yous all the way. That's the sort I don't mind. Now, I'd rather no one was in that field, of course, but if they must camp down there, then the polite ones are alright by me.

Anyway, ten minutes later, he's knocking again, just as I'm sitting down for my supper. Do you sell pegs? he asks. Come again? I says back. Pegs, tent pegs, can't find mine, he tells me. I thought about the old barn and the hundreds I had in there, on that back shelf. So I went down to the barn and came back up with a selection, so that he could pick out the ones he needed. Reasonable, see? When folk are polite, I am as well. Always willing to help out, as long as you do the same. So he picks out twelve and then he says, thanks very much, how much do I owe you? I was taken aback at first, I would've let him have them for nothing, that's what they cost me after all, but then I thought, just because he hadn't broken any rules so far didn't mean he wouldn't do later. He didn't look the sort to play loud music, but you never can tell, can you? Fifty pence I charged him. So six pound in total.

I put up the sign a week later and people soon started flocking in. 'Second-hand pegs for sale' it said, and they love all that, don't they? Recycling and doing their bit for the environment, even while they're charging about, trashing it to bits. The shrine to dad has taken a bit of a knock, of course, but he never liked a fuss anyway. He'd understand. Farming's a business, he knew that better than anyone. I've had to revise the list of punishments a little, too, because not everyone needed pegs, they kept asking what else we sold. And it's not fair, is it, taking two pegs off everyone when some of them deserved more. Different crimes, different punishments. You don't put people in prison for a parking fine, do you?

So I developed a system, a set of fines if you like. Turn up later than you told us you would, it's two pegs. Play loud music, five. Leaving a gate open is a walking sock, and two gates'll cost you both. Leave the campsite sink in a mess and I'll take a mug. Empty your pans in the grass, that costs you the pan. Pissing in the field at night costs you a head torch, letting your kids run around is a gas can. Just recently I increased the fine for leaving a gate open to one boot; nothing beats watching them hopping about in the mud, looking for it. No one ever thinks to ask if I've seen a boot lying anywhere. Idiots, the lot of them. We make more from the shop than we do from the campsite now, almost as much as from people staying in my house. People'll buy anything if they think it's recycled, the tattier the better. Like this couple I've got in here now. They've been looking through the walking sticks – the fine for leaving the toilets in a mess – for a quarter-hour now. Keep asking me which one they should buy, how they work. The man, he even asked me how long they should be. Same length as your leg, you bloody moron. Looks like he's made his mind up, though. Here he comes, grinning like a chump.

'We'll take these ones, then.'

Right you are.

'Unless you'd recommend something else?'

No, I wouldn't.

'It's a great selection you have here. And we like to know that the profit goes back into the community, that's exactly how it should be.'

It's 100% profit in here, my friend. Your thirty quid is going straight in my back pocket.

'OK, well, we're staying in the campsite, so I expect we'll see you up bright and early in the morning!'

You may do, you may not. Makes no odds to me.

Off they go, sticks in hand. And, wouldn't you know it, he doesn't say goodbye or thank you before leaving. Very rude. I'll be having that fleece hat off him, don't you worry. Nice bit of kit that. It'll fetch at least ten quid, I reckon.

12 The Adventure of the Missing Hosteller

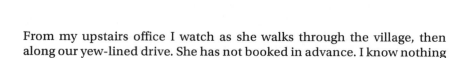

From my upstairs office I watch as she walks through the village, then along our yew-lined drive. She has not booked in advance. I know nothing about her.

I do, however, know Holmes' methods. I apply them.

Her backpack is full, extending above her head. If she is staying at a hostel, then she is not carrying a tent. Therefore she carries more with her than is needed to cross Dartmoor. A backpacker, moving from one place to the next. Elementary.

But from where?

An embroidered Australian flag is sewn onto the side of her pack. Possibly a memento from a visit there. But wait! It is a Crumpler, an Australian brand. The balance of probability suggests she is a resident of that country.

She is alone, which indicates single status; a woman who is discreet and of good reputation. And the fact she has not booked implies no fixed itinerary. It also confirms that the other hostel must be full. People only come here when the other place is full.

I head downstairs. By the time I am fully there, she is in the foyer, slouched on the bench nearest the door. She looks tired, her shoulders hunched forward, her head bowed. Her arms hang limply beside her. She must have travelled a long way, and that sinister moor is unforgiving. Small, too; short but also slender. Frail. Fragile.

She is still wearing her hiking boots, which shed detritus onto my carpet with her every movement. I do not like footwear inside. They leave marks, traces of every person who stays here.

'You have to leave your boots outside. In the rack.'

'Sorry, I didn't know.'

The accent is Australian. Watson would be proud of my deduction, although Holmes would undoubtedly deem it trifling.

'There is a sign. Above the door.'

'I guess I'll know for next time.'

Next time? This is highly improbable. No one ever stays here twice.

She's young: twenty-one or twenty-two. As one hand unties laces, the other withdraws a mobile telephone from her backpack. She flicks at it, no doubt selecting which photographs to add to social media accounts, where they can sit alongside the numerous and unimaginative shots of fish and chips, frothy beer and one hundred other English stereotypes to thrill those Neanderthal residents of her own country. They all do the same when they get here. It is a mystery why they think these pictures are significant.

But then Dartmoor is famous for its mysteries. How I wish Holmes were here now! He would solve that particular puzzle in an instant. One brief glance would be all he required to determine what they think and why they act in this herd-like way. He should have lived here, not London. Imagine how many of our legendary crimes would have been solved with him on the case! But no, he needed the capital with its crooks and its smog and his network of ragamuffin informers. He might have found life a little sedate here, it is true. Yet we could do with his genius now, as the mysteries continue apace. The curious incident of the Jenkins' hound, for instance, which has now been missing for close to three months.

My guest returns after correctly placing her boots on the rack outside. Hers are the only ones there, and it seems probable that she will be the only person staying tonight.

Apart from me. But then I am always here.

Five foot six, not more. She wipes muddy fronds of hair from her forehead, and her arms are spindly, with no muscle tone whatsoever. She is weaker than me, of that I am certain. Slightly built; one hundred and twenty-three pounds?

'You have to fill out a form. If you want to stay.'

'OK, sure.'

'I will get one for you.'

Alone. Foreign. People won't notice straight away, should she go missing. Not for a day or two. She did not book by phone or email, so it is possible no one even knows that she is here. She is perfect in every way. I will have to be friendlier, though, if I am to convince her to come with me. Friendly is not my natural state; I am aware that I do not always come across well with strangers. Furthermore, if she is tired then she may not want to head outside again. As I collect a form from the reception desk, I glance through the window. The afternoon clouds have shifted and the sky is fair. The weather is on my side, it seems. I consider what might be a friendly thing to say, but when I return she is gone.

I track her down in the kitchen, staring at the painting on the wall.

'Is that the Grimpen Mire?'

There is no need to reply. The title beneath the picture is quite clear. Why would anyone label a painting falsely?

'I love those Sherlock programmes.'

I glare at her from behind. That interminable series does the man absolutely no justice at all. It is a vile, showy stain upon his legacy, one that will be difficult to scrub away. I watched them filming an episode near here and considered all manner of ways to stop them. Alas, the security was ample and I am not as deft as Holmes in the art of disguise. Even Watson might have done better!

'Is it near here? I read on your website it's near here.'

'Two point four-six miles away.' I can feel my breath shortening, each exhalation catching as it escapes. This is almost too good to be true.

'I'd love to see it.'

'I can... I can show you.'

'Really? That'd be awesome.'

'I will need to collect my boots.'

'Cool, I'll wait here.'

'And you will have to put yours back on. Outside.'

'No worries.'

'You will also need your backpack with you.' It cannot be left here. Someone might see it; see that she was here.

'I thought you said it's only two miles away?' she asks.

'Two point four-six miles.'

'OK, whatever.'

Back in the upstairs office, I locate the tablets in my desk drawer. They are to help me sleep, but also serve to soothe my nerves when things become too much. I take one, sip water, sit. Another picture of the mire is on the wall opposite – but this one I keep for myself. It shows Stapleton's final moments as the moor consumes him, Holmes and Watson watching on. It is inaccurate, of course; Stapleton was alone out there, and the hound, which lurks on the far side in the picture, was already dead by this point. The sky is shown as clear, too, with stars sparkling, when in fact there was a thick fog on that fateful night. But despite these multiple discrepancies, I adore it. It captures the anger of the moor so perfectly; all of its unforgiving hunger is on display. It is not as treacherous as Watson claims; he exaggerated, as he was prone to do. But there are certainly pockets out there that will take a creature, consume it, take it down to a world from which it will not return. You just need to know where to find them.

The tablet has done as it should. I am ready. And I must make haste, before she changes her mind. I take one last look at my picture, the scene to which we are heading, then close the office door after picking up my own boots. Mine are allowed inside, of course. I always clean them before entering the hostel. Thoroughly.

His voice booms out before I reach the kitchen.

'Hey mate, Jackie was saying you guys're going onto the moor. Alright if I tag along?'

Another Australian. I stare at the hand he is stretching out towards me.

'Jackie and me, we met over in Newquay. She said she was heading this way, so I thought, why not join her?'

'You haven't booked.'

'Doesn't look like you're too busy, though.' He laughs, but it is not funny. The girl is smiling too, which displeases me.

'I have a migraine,' I say. To her. 'We cannot go.'

'So what are the boots for, mate?'

He laughs again. I want to slash him with each of the knives that sit on the counter, but they are all too blunt to do sufficient damage. Nor am I certain I could overpower him. I estimate his weight to be one hundred and forty-six pounds, possibly one hundred and forty-seven. He outweighs me by approximately fourteen pounds. The odds are unfavourable.

'You will have to complete the booking forms in the morning. Both of you.'

I rush up the stairs, my breath frantic, rattling, urgent. In the office, I lunge for my chair before my legs betray me. The tablets are still on the desk and I force one down in a dry swallow. Shame, shame, shame. Holmes never reacted to setbacks in this manner. No, he fought fire with fire! Even Watson would have done better. He was a little slow, a little clumsy, but by God he was brave! I need friend Watson to help me, but all I have are my tablets. Maybe I should try cocaine. Ha! But the thought of the Australians together disgusts me. I cannot stay here tonight, I need to get out. I locate my sleeping bag, then depart via the back door, unable to bear seeing them again. Look at me, skulking out of my own hostel. Shame, shame, shame.

It takes me thirty-six minutes to reach the mire. I often come here in the evenings, when I have had a troubling day. I know I will not be disturbed at this hour; only hardy men cross the moor at night. I head directly for my sleeping spot, a goyal on the mire's westward side that keeps off the worst of the wind, diverting it over you as it whistles across the moor. The land where it sits is slightly raised, keeping me out of the dank and mud that gathers in the hollows further down. I have slept here many times when my mind needs to be alone. The moor can be overrun with intruders during the day, those curious peasants who afflict it, but at night it is mine.

Holmes was, for once, incorrect about the moor. It is not desolate nor lifeless; rather, it attracts beasts of all kinds, each seeking its own peace and solitude. And this is their time. A barn owl swoops past, although its domain is the fields below so it has no business here. I like the moor best in these dark hours when the settled order of nature returns, when the powers of evil are exalted. I shuffle into my sleeping bag, then take one more tablet. This backpacker, and more specifically her pursuer, are a three-tablet problem.

The moon is not full, but sufficient to pick out the curves of the land and make the bulrushes around the mire shimmer. I stare, thinking about what is in there.

It was rabbits at first. The first one was injured, weak and already close to death. But it was too light; the wretched thing would not sink. It almost crawled off before I pushed it in with a stick. The other rabbits were healthier. Friskier. They took longer but also required my assistance to succumb.

The hound was next. A foul thing, smaller than any that ever mortal eye has rested upon. Yet loud and excitable. Westies are the worst kind of breed and this specimen deserved its fate, stupid beast that it was. Mrs Jenkins was distraught, naturally, which made it all the more worthwhile, considering the way she has treated me all these years. But dogs are tricky. People miss dogs and they make a lot of noise as they go. This one was a devil's agent of flesh and blood. It too needed assistance.

Sheep are far superior. The first one wandered by when I happened to be up here, and was too stupid to run away as most of its kind will do. It took forty-four minutes to disappear, but to my delight it did so unaided. I watched as it kicked, slipped, panicked, crying desperately for help, before eventually conceding defeat. Three more have since joined it, each performing a similar dance as the mire takes them down. It is the eyes that I relish the most: you can see the exact moment when they give up the fight. There's a delicious resignation as they realise this is their end. Folk say sheep are stupid, but they understand some things. Yes, the sheep were wonderful, but I need more. Something bigger. Something that can tell me its thoughts as it succumbs.

While sleep eludes me, I concentrate on the puzzle at hand. Her pursuer must be eliminated, but in a way that does not startle her, else risk her fleeing. She must not be aware he has gone, either, or she will refuse to accompany me here. Forcing her to come here is not an option: it is too far – two point four-six miles – to drag a person. No, she must do so willingly. Yet as the sun finally reaches my side of the tor, I am still unsure how to proceed.

Time is now against me, I realise, noting the sounds of the world coming alive: farm vehicles, cows, a car speeding on the road to Dartmeet. If I do not make haste, she will be gone before I return. I walk quickly, taking only thirty-three minutes, and at the front door I place my boots against the outside wall to dry. This is important: the mud is more easily removed when dry, meaning less risk of scratching the leather when cleaning. Next, I pick up the iron poker from beside the fireplace, ashamed that I must fall back upon the tools of a ruffian to resolve my problem.

He is in the kitchen. Alone. He looks up as I appear in the doorway.

'She left, mate. Said she had to get away. Dunno where she's going either, she didn't tell me.'

I say nothing, digesting this information as he slurps down cereal like a clogged drain.

'Nothing happened, in case you're wondering. Thought I'd try my luck again, but the same result as in Newquay. Nothing doing.' A shrug, then he shovels more wet food into his mouth. 'I'll probably leave myself in a bit. Not even told my mates I'm here. I guess I knew she was a long shot.'

I nod. She was far too special for him. For either of us. I stare at the painting on the wall: the mire, empty and alone. Holmes is absent from that one. How I wish he was here now, to stop these terrible things happening. To stop people like me.

'That's the Grimpen Mire, isn't it?' he asks, following my gaze. I do not reply. The title beneath the picture is, naturally, still there. 'Worth seeing before I head off?'

I study him, properly. He is bigger than me, but there is little muscle on the forearms.

He has not booked.

He has not told anyone where he is.

It is not yet eight in the morning. There is still some time before the first of the peasants reach my place on the moor.

'So what d'you think, mate? You up for showing me the moor?'

The only other person who knows he was here will not, it appears, trouble herself to look for him. One hundred and forty-six pounds, nothing more. Heavy enough for the mire to take him easily, yet his arrogance means he will put up a fight.

It should be a very rewarding struggle. Fifty-four minutes, I predict.

'I can take you there. Bring your backpack with you.'

13 Rambling Man

Douglas sighed loudly to no one as he filled his Thermos. Through the kitchen window he could see the secateurs reluctantly lent to his neighbour three days earlier. They lay on the dewy grass, almost hidden in swirls of unraked leaves. He had little doubt they'd been there the whole time, and would certainly need oiling when he got them back. If he got them back. His spade had never been returned – eventually he'd been forced to buy another. He hadn't brought that up, though, when the request for the secateurs had been made. He didn't like to make a fuss.

Shaking his head, he wrapped two slices of ginger cake in cling film and assessed some pears. Too firm. Instead he picked out the two bananas with fewest brown spots, placing them carefully in tea towel-lined Tupperware to minimise bruising in transit. After placing these goods on top of the rolled-up fleece in his rucksack, he checked again that his map and compass were in the top pocket. He hadn't used either for years, but the thought of being anywhere near the hills without them filled him with sufficient horror to check every time. There they were, as he'd known all along.

His boots, stuffed neatly with newspaper, were left in the hallway this time. Two faithful old servants, but not needed today. Which was a shame: the weather was perfect and the moors would be even more glorious than usual. The trees were assuming their bronchial winter form, and the overnight frost would make the mud along the paths crunch pleasingly underfoot. Maybe he'd climb Roseberry Topping tomorrow, although the weather was set to change overnight. He'd have to set off early as well. The hill was increasingly overrun these days, even in bad weather, and you had to time it right to avoid the crowds. The rest of the North York Moors weren't much better, either. The villages along the railway line had long since been ruined by fans of that infernal TV programme. Groups completing the Coast to Coast were the worst of the lot though, hooting and hollering as if they were the first ones to have ever done it, never mind the hundredth that week. It had been very different when Douglas did it. The route was the same, but everything else had changed.

Ravanelli, the creaky old Labrador, was waiting by the front door. He'd had a frustrating morning, being tormented and ignored by next door's cat. He followed slowly and when he finally reached the car, Douglas gave him a gentle shove up into the boot. Man's best friend, so people said. He didn't believe it himself as he and the dog hadn't exactly hit it off. That had happened to Douglas a lot during his life. Fifty-nine, single, and with few people he'd rank above 'acquaintance'. He was meeting one of those few today, though.

Before starting the engine, Douglas made one additional check, one not part of his usual routine. He patted the top pocket of his fleece, just to be certain that today's additional item was there. It was, of course. He removed the small red box from his pocket and opened it. Not a dazzling ring, nor expensive, but he was hopeful she would like it.

Douglas tutted as the car headed along the high street. If it wasn't for Elizabeth, he'd have left this place years ago. It had been home for all but three of his fifty-nine years, yet he liked it less now than ever. Half the shops had closed and those still open were ones he never visited... betting shops and coffee chains, cheap bakeries and discount stores. Nor did he like the ugly new estate that had sprung up at the far end, built in a style that bore not so much as a nod toward the town's architectural traditions. He smiled as he passed the school in which he'd spent well over half of his days on earth, first as a pupil, then as a teacher. Not for the memories of the years spent teaching – he'd failed to glean much enjoyment from being trapped in that pit of noise and germs and oppressive central heating – but because it was the first place he'd ever seen her. And, moments later, fallen in love. He'd confessed as much to his older brother that evening and been scorned for it – 'you're twelve, you don't know what it even means' – but Douglas had known what he felt. And still felt, forty-seven years later.

Not that he'd suffered in silence: this was a love that had dared to speak its name on several occasions. On her fourteenth birthday, he'd presented her with a handmade card and a book he just knew she'd love. She'd laughed at him, walking off with two friends who were quick to join in with her scorn. Two years later, he'd opted for the safer approach of going to her house with a gift. She hadn't laughed then, but neither had she invited him inside, nor reciprocated the gesture on his own birthday a few weeks later.

Douglas had left, reluctantly, to study biochemistry in Newcastle, relying on his mother to keep him updated on who Elizabeth was seen with. Back during university holidays he'd done that himself, spending his evenings seeing where she went, who she talked to, and for how long. Creepy? No, he was a trainee scientist undertaking vital research in preparation for the day he'd come home for good. Simply being rigorous, as he always had been.

On the day of his return after graduating, Douglas had gone straight to her house to ask her out. Properly. Dinner somewhere smart, maybe dancing, and he wouldn't take no for an answer. Her mother had opened the door and offered a warm smile – she'd always liked Douglas – and told him Elizabeth was out with Alan, but perhaps he could come round another evening, it would be lovely to hear about Newcastle, about his studies, how's your mother doing, do send her my regards. Douglas spent the following two weeks investigating Alan. Early results revealed him to be an overweight smoker who worked for one of the chemical companies over in Redcar. Further research would be needed to establish quite what Elizabeth saw in him, but the early hypothesis was money. Given that he didn't have any of his own with which to compete, Douglas had decided to take a little more time to consider his next move.

The wedding invitation had arrived soon afterwards, evening reception only. He'd replied immediately, thank you, sorry, can't make it, and then urgently set about finding a plausible reason why he couldn't go. The first thing he spotted in the newspaper was a two-week walking holiday completing the Coast to Coast path with the local rambling club. He booked a place immediately, anything to ensure he was nowhere nearby on the wedding day. The other side of the country was still too close, but as far as he could afford.

The first week had been horrendous. Rain hammered his body by day, and at night his mind was ravaged with images of the happy couple on their honeymoon. But, by the second week, the sun had jostled the rain aside and he had, despite his best efforts, started to enjoy the repetitive rhythms of each day – cooking breakfast, checking his kit, studying the route for the day. He'd even become aware of his fellow walkers, going so far as to talk to them when absolutely necessary. He'd refused to join them in dipping feet into the sea at Robin Hood's Bay, despite their protestations that he must; he hadn't taken part in the ritual at St Bees and saw little reason to do so at the finish. But he'd realised, while watching his new companions splash in the water, that he might just have found something to distract him from his pain. Those two weeks marked the start of a new love affair, albeit one that came a very distant second to his first. Before long, walking was the focus of his life. And Douglas was good at it. He excelled at navigation, he knew how to prepare for all weathers, and always turning up stocked with energy and perseverance.

People who are good at sports end up playing for better teams. Those with musical talent might form a band. And if you're good at walking? You climb the ranks of your local rambling society. Unable to even contemplate trying to find someone to replace Elizabeth, Douglas threw himself wholeheartedly into their activities. First he offered to lead the weekend walks. Within a year he became membership secretary and treasurer soon afterwards. When Eric Batley announced he was stepping down as chairman, no one even considered standing against Douglas in the vote. He was pleased, relieved even – anything to keep his mind off Elizabeth.

Clocks tick. Years pass. The town wasn't big and Douglas was unable to avoid them completely, despite his best efforts. A quick hello while shopping, a brief chat at the church fete. In his early thirties, their oldest daughter started at his school and the second daughter quickly followed. He'd been relieved that neither ended up in his classes, knowing he'd have been unable to decide between favouring them because they were hers, or picking on them because they were Alan's. Yet the occasional sight of her around the school – parents' evenings, school plays – had provided unwelcome reminders of the life he'd missed out on, simply by acting too late.

By his forties, Douglas had settled into such a steady routine – teaching five days, walking two – that it was a significant, albeit welcome, shock when Elizabeth turned up for one of his weekend walks. Then another, a few weeks later. She wasn't a regular, not at first. But as the girls grew older and increasingly filled their weekends with things that didn't involve her, she had started coming to all of them. During a walk around Bransdale – one of his shorter routes at a little under six miles, but always popular – she confided that she and Alan hardly spent any time together any more. Douglas had been thrilled to discover this, a sensation only heightened when she had agreed to help him plan the walking programme for the following year.

Douglas chuckled as he drove past the Portakabin on the edge of town that served as the club's headquarters. He often wondered where he'd spent more time: in there or on the hills. Yet he liked the draughty old hut. He had plenty of happy memories of evenings spent there with Elizabeth, plotting future excursions. And she'd been exactly what they'd needed, setting up a website to attract new members and gently encouraging the regulars to travel further afield. It was Elizabeth who had persuaded them, despite fierce protestations, to add trips to the Dales to their programme. Douglas had also resisted at first – he had little time for the Dales, far too flashy and expensive for his tastes – but quickly relented when she explained the trips would take full weekends. The chance to spend nights with her, albeit in separate rooms, had been too much to resist, and he'd always made sure their rooms were at least adjacent. And they worked well as a team: she found comfortable yet affordable places to stay, while he researched routes away from the overcrowded honeypots. The annual trips to Raydale, Arkengarthdale and Coverdale quickly became highlights of the club's summer programme.

By the time they were heading into their fifties, Douglas and Elizabeth were firm friends – confidants even. Her daughters had left home and Alan was often away on business; he was, by that time, on the board of the chemical company, the reward for a lifetime of loyalty. They'd never had any shared interests, she'd confessed to Douglas one evening over a drink. Hardly even a couple any more, she'd said, just two people sharing a house. Douglas listened that night to the story of a marriage drifting towards its conclusion, wondering how much longer he should be the shoulder to cry on and when he should suggest that she left Alan. That was surely the time, but he couldn't quite bring himself to say it. He had reasoned that it was better to let things reach their natural conclusion.

Douglas had little belief in fate or providence, but all the same it felt significant that Alan's illness was diagnosed the very next day. Douglas wasn't callous enough to wish him an early death, but bitterly resented the toll it took on Elizabeth. The constant care Alan needed took up all her time... washing, feeding, exercises, hospital visits, more washing, shopping, getting him out of bed, getting him back into it, walking the dog. There had been little time for any rambling, never mind helping him organise club activities. The members were understanding, naturally, and everyone missed her. But no one had missed her as much as Douglas.

He couldn't remember when he'd first suggested helping out, but soon enough he was coming around every Tuesday and Thursday at noon. He had plenty of spare time having gone part-time at fifty – partly due to tightening staff budgets, but mostly due to his dislike of the students. He sat with Alan to give Elizabeth some time to be 'normal', if only for a few hours. Douglas would have preferred to spend the time with her, of course, but took comfort in knowing he was helping. He had even warmed to Alan slightly, albeit from a glacial starting point. They never became friends but, over the years, established a comfortable, almost wordless routine of tea, crosswords and afternoon TV. On Mondays (two afternoons a week had quickly become all five), Douglas read out the weekend football reports, always starting with 'Boro of course. After that the racing results, then local news, followed by a joint assault on the cryptic crossword. Alan was usually asleep in his chair by the time Elizabeth got home, giving her a few precious minutes to tidy the house before they woke him together for the evening routine of washing and getting him back upstairs.

At the end, Alan barely needed to tap at death's door for it to swing open for him. Douglas had been there when it happened, patting Alan's hand gently as Elizabeth wept on the opposite side of the bed. Two years ago now, Douglas realised as he turned the car into her road. He'd known there would need to be a dignified pause, time to allow for whatever grieving she needed to do for a man she had long since stopped loving. There was also the need to consider what people might think, what they might say. About her, of course, he wasn't bothered what they thought of him, and never had been. He knew people respected him more than liked him, if they ever thought about him at all. What was there to think about? Few people grow up with dreams of teaching biology in the same school for thirty-plus years, or spending their evenings doing the admin for a medium-sized rambling club. So he had waited, then waited a bit more. There was no guidance in these matters, and no one he could ask about what would be a respectful period. But he had decided, one week ago, that now was the right time. Now or never.

Or rather, now or any time in the next four to six months.

Elizabeth hadn't told him about her own illness. He'd overheard two women in the town's supermarket, and there had been no question of who they were discussing. Had that prompted him to buy the ring? Possibly. After dallying for most of his life, the matter was now somewhat pressing.

'Did you bring Ravanelli?' Elizabeth asked excitedly, as he manoeuvred her carefully into the passenger seat.

'Of course; he's in the boot,' Douglas replied.

'How's he doing? Is he eating better?'

'He's fine,' he reassured her. He wasn't; the vet had confirmed that Ravanelli's tumour was incurable. Douglas was a little relieved; he didn't much care for the dog. But another part of him willed it to outlast Elizabeth, so he wouldn't have to give her the news about her beloved pet. Ravanelli let out a low grumble from the boot, helping to keep up the pretence that everything was the same as it ever was.

'My grandson's having his appendix out,' Elizabeth continued as they headed south out of town.

Douglas said nothing. He didn't like hearing about her grandchildren. Grandchildren made him think of her children, whose existence meant that she must have... with Alan...

'Where do you want to go today?' he asked quickly, shaking an unpleasant image from his mind. 'I thought a bit of sea air might do you good.' Sea air didn't cure cancer, Douglas knew that, although it couldn't hurt. But he knew exactly where she'd want to go. The same place she always did when he took her out.

'Can we go to Roseberry? I'd like to sit on our bench. It'll be looking wonderful today.'

Douglas smiled. Roseberry Topping had always been her favourite, the same as his. Ravanelli would be pleased, too, as he could sit beneath the bench and wait for any scraps that dropped within his arthritic reach.

'Can you turn the heating up a little, Dougie?'

He slid the button all the way to the right.

'That's too much.'

He moved it halfway back.

'Yes, that's just right.'

'You're like all three bears in one, you are,' he said. She laughed, and Douglas allowed himself a smile. In the car park, he reassembled her wheelchair and gently helped her into it. It was an effort to push her up the rutted track to the bench, but he didn't mind. Douglas looked, as always, in quiet awe of the sight before them. The hill was resplendent in its autumn coat, and he envied the walkers who were swarming its flanks like brightly coloured ants attacking a fallen ice lolly. Two men were racing up. Why come out for a walk and then rush to get it over with? Douglas hadn't hurried in his life. He preferred taking his time. And he could tell, even from this distance, that few of them were sticking to the paths, despite the numerous signs instructing them to do so. Still, what could you do with people these days? They were probably leaving their rubbish up there as well, assuming that someone else would pick it up for them. Tutting to himself, he spread the rug out carefully on the bench, then tucked another over her legs. Next, he placed the Thermos, cake and fruit between them.

'Which tea do you want? I bought the herbal ones you like, or the decaffeinated.'

'Herbal, please.'

'Right you are.'

Douglas poured hot water into the cups and began unwrapping the cake.

'It's a wonderful hill, isn't it?' she sighed. 'Such a perfect shape.'

'Maybe we can try it next week,' he said, after a moment's thought. 'If we leave a bit earlier, I could push you up there, I think. Not to the top, but a little way up, I'm sure. The dog'll have to stay at home, mind, I can't be looking after both of you.'

'You'll have to excuse me next week, Dougie, I'll be on my honeymoon.'

He paused, a piece of cake halfway to his mouth. Honeymoon? Despite their many years of friendship, he'd never really been in tune with her sense of humour, and this one passed him by as well.

'Heading somewhere nice, are you?'

'Only Whitby.' She placed a frail hand on his cake-free one. 'It's Eric, Eric Batley. We've become very close. I've been visiting him at the home. He asked me two weeks ago. You know him, don't you?'

Douglas did indeed. Eric Batley, his predecessor as chairman at the rambling club. An acquaintance rather than a friend, but Douglas had still helped to move his things to the care home, after it had been agreed that Eric had had one fall too many in his own place. A whole day he'd been driving back and forth, ferrying Eric's possessions for him. What was that, six weeks ago? It couldn't be much longer.

'Doesn't hang about, does he?'

'I guess you don't at our age. I would have invited you, but we decided on just family.'

'I see.'

'And you never came to my first one.'

'No, I didn't.'

They watched a young family heading slowly up the main path, the littlest member falling repeatedly. Douglas suspected it was on purpose, so the dad would carry her to the top. He tried to work out how often he'd been up there himself; at least thirty times a year, for the best part of forty years. What was that, a hundred and twenty times? No, wait a minute, one thousand two hundred. Had he really walked up the same hill more than a thousand times?

'I was going to ask you, you know,' he said quietly.

Elizabeth didn't reply, but he knew she had heard. Her lungs may be failing, but her hearing was just fine. Douglas wondered if there would be a response of any kind. He studied his slice of cake, anything to avoid having to look at her. He couldn't, not with wet eyes. Up on the hill, the mother was taking the little child down, while dad and the older one pushed on for the top.

'I'm a lucky woman, you know. I've had one happy marriage – and it was happy, for many years – and now I might have another. And I've always had you looking out for me. Ever since we were teenagers.'

'Twelve. We were twelve when we met.'

Douglas had never once thought that he was the love of her life, but nor was Alan. He doubted Eric was either. People married whoever they were with when they wanted to get married. It was timing that meant she married Alan instead of him, nothing more than that. He hadn't been around at the right moment. But to miss out a second time? Once was bad luck, but this time the blame really did fall squarely at his feet. Too long spent dithering, trying to do the decent thing. And once again he'd been outpaced, this time by someone who could no longer even walk. A gust of wind burst the tear on his cheek and blew it away.

'I'd like to go to the Dales when I'm back,' she said. 'Semer Water. I'd like to see Semer Water one last time.'

This time Douglas pretended not to hear.

'You always liked Raydale, didn't you?' she continued. 'You told me once it was your favourite dale. As much as you could bring yourself to have a favourite "over there". But I know why. You always like the quiet spots best.' She squeezed his hand. 'Let's go, just you and me. Eric won't mind.'

Maybe I mind, Douglas thought, snatching his hand away. What am I, a taxi driver for the dying? She was Eric's responsibility now. It was a race to the finish line for those two, he thought bitterly. Those three, if you included the dog. Angry with her for the first time in forty-seven years, he studied the hill intensely. The father and son had reached the summit and Douglas could see the man fiddling with a GPS. On Roseberry Topping, for goodness' sake; only a fool could get lost up there, but there were plenty of them about. He couldn't stand those things; what use were they when the batteries went? No, it was map and compass for him, always had been. He decided he would definitely climb it tomorrow, whatever the weather was up to.

'Alright, Semer Water,' he sighed.

'Thank you, Dougie.' She moved her hand alongside his and he patted it gently; he wanted to hold it, but it didn't seem right. Not under the circumstances.

'And you'll look after Ravanelli for me, won't you? When I'm gone?'

This would have been an opportune moment for the dog to place a pleading paw on Douglas's leg, or even just nudge him affectionately. But instead he just sat there, watching the slice of ginger cake and willing it to drop. Douglas tutted and broke off a piece.

'I suppose so,' he muttered, giving the dog the rest of his cake, along with a pat between the ears. Unwittingly, he reached for the pocket of his jacket. The ring was still in there, but he had no idea what he was going to do with it now.

14 Pine Marten vs Racoon

The smaller mustelids – weasels, stoats, martens – are the wildlife photographer's best friend. Bold little creatures, they rarely show fear around humans, carrying out their business with little more than a glance towards any oversized observers. They're mostly active in the early hours when, as even a novice knows, the light is at its best. Most importantly, they are rare. In an age when anyone with a smartphone thinks their photographs are worth sharing with the world, mustelids offer that increasingly elusive quality: novelty. These tiny tubular mammals are not captured just by being out and about; the photographer has to put in many long, cold hours waiting to get their shot.

Which is exactly why Frances finds herself slipping about in snow-flecked mud somewhere on the slopes that stretch between Ben A'an and Loch Katrine. It is a setting sufficiently hostile to see off all except the most determined photographers, but Frances certainly qualifies on that count. Especially now, when the prize on offer – Wildlife Photographer's best amateur, 'British mammals' category – is surely hers, if only she can capture a mustelid. While any sort would be a welcome addition to her portfolio, she is desperate for a pine marten, a specimen even more splendid than its taxonomical cousins, thanks to its rich colours and vivid markings.

There are none about, though. Not that she is able to find. Since six o'clock she's been braving treacherous mica schist and the piercing chill of a Scottish morning. Moving as unobtrusively as possible with a large camera and a bag brimming with equipment, she has been following, with increasing frustration and no little bruising, the route that she was promised would bring rewards. The night porter had offered: 'Follow the burn by the gate up to the ridge, then head towards the loch. People always see them up there; you can't miss them.'

Can't miss them. Advice all too easily dispensed from the comfort of a reception desk, but much trickier to realise in the army of thick pines that permit little warmth or daylight into the world beneath. The beasts could scoot past right in front of her and she'd fail to spot them, focused as she is on keeping her footing. Of course, a second pair of eyes would help. Ideally, they would belong to Roger, for if any eyes could locate an elusive species hidden in a forest, it is those belonging to Britain's third-best wildlife photographer (according to the Natural History Museum).

Nor would Frances object to his company. Wildlife photographers are silent by necessity, but Roger complements near-wordlessness with oodles of rugged moodiness, which Frances admires even more than his skill behind the lens. And she is so, so close to the ultimate reward: two weeks of expert guidance amid the grand mountainscape of Yellowstone, to capture North America's finest beasts for a feature-length spread in Britain's leading wildlife photography magazine – and all the while benefiting from Roger's close supervision. Very close, Frances hopes. There is widespread online gossip among the denizens of photography chatrooms about Roger's preferred evening activities on such trips – rumours he does little to dissuade – and she yearns for that even more than exposure in the magazine. She's made it to the final three; all she needs is something extra special to ensure her portfolio is the one selected. All she needs is a pine marten.

Roger would have found one by now, of that she's certain. But Roger, who is generously spending two days with each finalist (their reward for making it onto the shortlist) is currently somewhere between Ben A'an and Inverness. Soon after they arrived last night, he took a phone call. Listening in as well as she could, Frances gleaned that a minke whale had been spotted near Lossiemouth. He set off straight away, a long drive in the dead of night being of little inconvenience to the professional. Her generous offer to accompany him was declined.

At ten o'clock, she concedes defeat, for now at least. The blasted creatures will have taken refuge for the day, their hunt for breakfast concluded. Even if they were to peek out from their tree-bound hideaways, the light breaking through the trees is all wrong for the standout shot she needs. Slowly, carefully, she picks a route back down towards the hotel, feeling frustrated in any number of ways.

Round one to the martens.

The night porter is nowhere to be seen, thus avoiding Frances' recriminations. Instead, she decides on a restorative coffee in the hotel's luxurious lounge, and asks the waitress for a shot of whisky to be added.

Something to take the edge off the chill, she jokes, even though she makes the same request all year round. Retiring to the large maroon sofa by the log fire, she picks over her failure. Any photographer can have a bad day when that all-important quality of luck is absent, but she cannot afford another. There are only two more opportunities, this evening and tomorrow morning. She could, of course, complain to the magazine's editor about being entitled to a second guided session, given her expert tutor was absent for much of the first. But Roger is the editor... And, as he's also one of the competition judges, it seems prudent to keep on his good side until the winner is announced. She is confident it will be her – her list of amateur awards is almost as long as her most expensive lens – but this is the big one, and without a marten, there is the increasing worry of her portfolio falling agonisingly short. Self-doubt rears up as the finish line draws near. She has some superb shots – the boxing hares in the morning dew remains her favourite – but still lacks an image that instantly reveals her intuition, her ability to spot and capture what others miss. Sipping her enhanced coffee, Frances ponders if there is another British mammal that could stand in for a pine marten.

'I'm tellin' ya, girl, it's a racoon.'

'Honey, they don't have racoons in Britain, I keep saying.'

'An' I keep sayin', it's a damn racoon!'

'Here, lemme ask someone. Excuse me, miss, can we ask you a question?'

Frances hunkers lower into the sofa, hoping that the two Americans she avoided eye contact with upon entering the lounge are talking to someone else. A tap on her shoulder confirms the worst.

'Excuse me, miss, can we ask you something? My husband, that's Wade over there, he took a photo this morning and we were wondering, what sort of animal it is.'

The woman leans over the back of the sofa, smiling sweetly and holding out a camera. Frances smiles back with what little warmth she can muster. Answering their query seems the easiest way to end this unwelcome intrusion, and she skims rapidly through the images on the display screen. They are the standard output of the over-eager hobbyist with a lens more expensive than they know what to do with: all close-ups of Scottish animals, but nothing remarkable and the focal point never where it should be.

'There. That one there. It ain't a racoon, is it?'

Frances stares the image. She wants to scream, to hurl the device through the window, into the fire, against this stupid woman's stupid head.

'It's a pine marten,' she confirms, zooming in to study it in detail. It's incredible: expertly focused, beautifully composed and capturing perfectly the marten's essence. It is a truly remarkable shot.

'Martin? Like the boy's name?' asks the woman.

'With an 'e.'

'See, honey? It ain't a racoon, I told you.' The woman beams triumphantly across at her husband.

'I still say I'm right,' Wade replies, albeit at a reduced volume. 'Marten's what the English call a racoon, ain't it.'

It is a statement more than an enquiry and her rising fury prevents Frances from replying, either to confirm in the negative or point out they're actually in Scotland. As she scans around the digital image, Wade and his wife join her on the sofa.

'Isn't he an adorable little fella?'

'They're extremely aggressive, actually. It could bite your finger clean off.' Frances has half a mind to demonstrate how it might do this as the woman leans across her and taps the display screen.

'This little guy? I can't believe it. I love his creamy tux, like he's going to his high school prom!'

Begrudgingly, Frances chuckles. The pine marten certainly is a finely attired creature, and this one seems especially pleased with himself. Her instinctive affinity with any fellow nature-lover softens her tone just a touch. 'Yes, they are marvellous creatures. And you've captured it perfectly.'

'That one? Just a bit of luck, I guess,' says Wade, pride oozing out through the modesty.

'Wade just loves taking photographs, he's always out with his camera. And he goes to all the exhibitions in Cheyenne. That's where we're from, y'know. In Wyoming.'

'Congratulations,' Frances mutters, still fixated on the camera screen, her envy failing to subside.

'You never miss an exhibition, do you Wade?'

'I try my damnedest not to! Listen, miss, can we get you another coffee? Maybe while you tell us a little more about this marten fella.'

Frances doesn't respond, too focused as she is on the image before her. It's perfect. The marten's outline is framed by two frosted tussocks of grass, and is so clear you can count its individual whiskers, distinct against the crimson sunrise and the crenulations of the snow-capped Trossachs in the background. It's better than anything she has ever seen, never mind taken. With a humbling gulp Frances realises she wouldn't have even thought of this composition, let alone pulled it off. She could never have taken this shot herself.

'Miss? Can we get you another coffee?'

In an instant, Frances snaps back to the room.

'Let's order one from my room. I have a book about Scottish wildlife that might interest you.'

Upstairs, Frances digs out her book and the Americans, sitting side by side on her bed, pore over it. The coffee arrives and Frances signs the bill while the waitress places the tray carefully on the sideboard.

'Wow, look at those guys, Wade. Look at those antlers!'

'Ain't got nuthin' on an elk.'

'And oh my good gosh, I just love these otters! Where could we find them, miss?'

'Are you crazy, girl? We've got otters back home. Bigger ones than them, I'll say.'

Frances refuses to be drawn into a transatlantic otter-size showdown. 'Your best bet is to head for the coast if you want to see otters. Or one of the islands.'

'Wow, this is super-strong coffee!'

'That's how we drink it in Scotland.'

'An' what about these...?'

'Capercaillies,' Frances interjects quickly, to spare herself from having to hear her guests attempt the word. 'Try the Cairngorms, though they're notoriously hard to track down. Very rare.'

She patiently answers their questions about Scotland's wildlife, from the mundane to the ridiculous. At last, as she explains for the fourth time that wildcats are not just 'big house cats', it begins.

'Wade, honey, I don't feel so good.'

'Jeez, girl, I'm feelin' it too. I told ya, the food here ain't like back home. Too much grease.'

'Oh gee, oh gee, oh gee...'

Frances says nothing until she is certain of their next move.

'Gee, I'm so sorry miss, I think I've gotta go!'

'An' I'm damn sure needin' to go! C'mon girl!'

Her gamble that good manners and American pride will prevent them from asking to use her bathroom pays off. As they head down the corridor, she calls after them in a voice that expresses her best approximation of concern. 'Don't worry, I'll bring your camera to your room.'

She locks the door and swiftly copies that perfect image onto her laptop. Next, she removes everything from Wade's camera. There is a soupçon of guilt as she selects 'delete all', but knows her story will only be plausible if everything is wiped 'by accident'. She feels a further twinge at stealing someone else's photograph, but consoles herself with the fact that its previous owner didn't even know what the animal is called. And she feels no remorse about the caffeine tablets she slipped into their drinks. Frances always keeps some in her kit bag; they are essential for staying awake during long night-time shoots. She's never suffered the laxative effects of which the packet warns, but then she's never taken four at once, crushed into one cup of coffee. It will wear off shortly, so, apart from the loss of some treasured holiday snaps, this is a victimless crime.

Roger scrutinises the image once more, using the touchpad to zoom in and move around its pixelated form. He's sure it isn't hers – it's far too good, and too different from her usual efforts. He's seen her competition portfolio and she doesn't compose shots with this much imagination, never mind that she lacks the aperture control to contrast subject and background so sharply. The only reason she even made it this far is because he hasn't yet decided which of the all-female shortlist he intends to take with him to Yellowstone for two weeks of shagging and snapping. The two-day tuition sessions were a flash of inspiration; as any photographer knows, it's important to test out a piece of kit before taking it into the field. He doesn't want to be stuck out there with someone who isn't any good. Yet with this addition to her portfolio, it looks like it will be Frances. He doesn't know where she got this picture – the EXIF data confirms it was taken this morning, and from somewhere near the hotel – but it's definitely not hers. Whoever took it has talent. It is a truly stunning wildlife image, worthy of the rarest of photographic accolades: iconic.

'These are good,' he mutters. 'Especially this one of the marten.'

'Thank you,' smiles Frances, sitting up and pulling the bed cover around her, though her modesty has left the building. 'Do you think I'm in with a chance?'

'That's up to me and the other judges, isn't it?' he replies sharply. Annoyed that she's still awake despite his enthusiastic performance, because he doesn't want to have to go through it all again right now. He really needs her to be asleep.

She needs to go to sleep...

He turns around, clicking on a cute smile. 'But it's an excellent collection, one worthy of a celebratory toast. Champagne?'

Placing the camera carefully on the bed, he stands up and walks to the sideboard in her hotel room. Taking care to block her view with his naked body, Roger retrieves a bottle of sparkling wine from the minibar and divides it evenly in two small tumblers.

'Cheers!' he says, knocking his back and grinning to encourage his student to do likewise. 'We should head back out there this evening, you can show me exactly where you took them. Who knows, I might manage to take one almost as good!'

Roger sits on the bed and picks up the laptop again, and the picture of the marten against the sunrise. It's utterly remarkable, possibly as good as his own best work. 'What do you think, Frances? Shall we go out later for a shoot?'

When she fails to reply a second time, he leans over to check she is properly asleep. Like all professional photographers he keeps a supply of sleeping pills in the side pocket of his camera bag, just in case he can't drop off the night before an early start. He didn't expect them to work so quickly, but then he did add four to her wine. Coming so swiftly after a long bout of energetic sex, four were evidently enough.

Swiftly he copies the perfect image to his own laptop. Next, he deletes everything from hers. He feels no guilt as he selects the 'delete all' option, or for stealing her picture: he's positive she did the same, he just doesn't know where from. And this image is exactly what he needs for his forthcoming exhibition on British mammals, which will open in Cheyenne, Wyoming, as soon as he's done with that two-week tour in Yellowstone. He smiles at the neatness of his plan. There is absolutely no risk of anyone out there knowing how he got the image: he'd be amazed if any American even knows what a pine marten is. While Frances snores, he goes to the fridge and takes out the second bottle of sparkling wine. The photo he now possesses is deserving of its own toast.

15 Three Across, Nine Letters

'There is, of course, a scurrilous suggestion that he had no interest in the fells at all, and his regular jaunts around them were merely a cover for, shall we say, more romantic pursuits. But, as the man himself is no longer with us to defend his reputation, we'll leave it as that: a mere rumour. I'm Garth Winfried-Law, and I'd like to thank you all, wholeheartedly and one last time, for your warm welcome and even warmer attention. If you have any further questions, I'll be at the bar for as long as it remains open.'

The applause ripples at first, then crescendos as I walk across the hotel's pleasingly packed lounge. Perching on the stool I'd reserved with my trench coat, I remove the cravat and undo a button or two on my burgundy waistcoat. Business over; now for some pleasure. My black fedora on the bar is angled carefully so the pheasant feather tucked into its band faces outwards. That small feather is integral to my man-of-the-countryside image. The barmaid, a buxom redhead, smiles as she brings my pre-ordered double gin and tonic. I beam back, topping it off with a sly wink. She's chirpy and pretty enough to be a useful back-up option should my audience fail to proffer anything better. I've spotted a few potentials, but it's never easy to be sure with a dimly lit audience. I'll need to inspect the goods on offer close up before committing.

Soon enough they begin to shuffle over, arranging themselves according to eagerness, the keenest at the front. This is how every crowd reacts: Wainwright obsessives love talking about their hero as much as they adore hearing about him. Unfortunately, and once again true to the established pattern, it's a fan of the male variety who reaches me first. I'll plump for bachelor rather than divorcee, and happily wager ten pounds that his job involves admin of some kind. Further, I guess that fell walking is just one of several hobbies about which he obsesses. Trainspotting? A little too obvious, but model railways are a strong possibility.

'May I just thank you once more for an extremely informative talk, I enjoyed it immensely. I wanted to ask, and you probably get asked this all the time' – he actually chuckles here, bless him – 'you mentioned that Haystacks is Wainwright's favourite hill in the Lake District, which is of course well known, but I was wondering which is your own personal favourite?'

He's correct on both counts: not only about Alfred's preferred peak, but also about the clockwork monotony with which I am asked this question. Is it really all they can think of? I'm tempted, as always, to reply honestly: I don't have one, having never been up a single one of those rain-drenched volcanoes. But that's not what he wants to hear; it's not what any of them want to hear. And my duty, on this evening and every other, is to give the people what they want. Luckily, having been forced to plough through Alfred's interminable musings more than once in the name of research, I have several possible responses at my disposal.

'An excellent question, Mr...?'

'It's Shimmell, Colin Shimmell.'

'Well, Mr Shimmell, as mountain men like you and I know only too well, it's virtually impossible to pin it down to just one candidate. But' – I usually throw in a dramatic gesture at this point, an upraised finger or a thump on the bar – 'if you force my hand, then I would plump for one not too far from us right here in Grasmere. High Raise may not be remarkable in itself, but when approached via the enchanting Sourmilk Gill and the majestic Easedale Tarn, then I truly believe there is no finer day to be had in this green and pleasant land of ours. It was one of Alfred's favourites too, of course.'

I doubt very strongly that Sourmilk Gill is enchanting, or Easedale Tarn majestic; I'd wager a further ten pounds that both are, by contrast, cold and bleak and miserable. But I always opt for something nearby, wherever I am speaking, to provide myself with a moment of puerile amusement the next morning as I watch my audience, decked in their finest cagoules, dutifully trudge up whichever hill I have selected. They'll do anything to feel that little bit closer to their idol, even if it is via the medium of a self-appointed Wainwright expert. I take an extended sip from my drink, one large enough to drain it in fact, and beam at the crowd. They are now all huddling around me, like sheep at a stile.

'And, Mr Shimmell, what would be at the peak of your own list?'

'Call me Colin, please. It might be boring, but Haystacks is my favourite too.'

Of course, another Haystacks zealot. It's incredible, their devotion to abiding by every last whim of a long-dead curmudgeon none of them ever met.

'Not at all, Colin,' – it is, very boring – 'Haystacks is a tremendous little hill, and would very possibly sneak into second place on my list, tied with old Saddleback herself, Blencathra. But I cannot fault your selection. You and Alfred share excellent taste.'

He glows at this personal association with the man of the hour and points to my empty glass. With another rich smile I confirm, yes, I would love a refill, then scan the flock for someone else to ask me an utterly pointless and unimaginative question. So lacking in wit are they that not five minutes pass before another enquires as to my favourite fell. But, amid their bleating, there are numerous offers of drinks and I soon have four glasses awaiting my attention, each enlivened with a rugged slice of two-week-old lemon. More importantly, I have identified my prize ewe for the night.

It started with an anagram... Year Nine drama students from the arse end of a nowhere town placed few demands on a supply teacher who let them do as they please. I usually resorted to solving cryptic crosswords while the rabble violated Shakespeare, until the day when three across – 'Whence Wainwright got his needle(s)?' – finished the puzzle early, leaving me without distraction until the end of the lesson except for an idle investigation on the classroom computer. The man himself provided little of interest, the miserable old sod, but I was astounded to see how many appreciation societies he had spawned. A vague idea became a solid plan...

All actors long to be on the stage, even amateurs such as myself and, with no interesting offers forthcoming – no offers at all, if the truth be told – I decided upon a solo tour. Anything to offset the tedium that is the world of the underemployed supply teacher. Anything to avoid having to watch television in a tiny flat assailed by noises and smells emanating from the takeaway below.

An A-level student created the website for me in return for a bottle of tequila and a grade A in his mocks. It's a simple format, just a photo of mountains and an online contact form. The boy even wrote a series of fake reviews for me, bless him. People contact me via the online form and, if it sounds promising, I ring them back and agree a date. I'm booked almost every weekend: there is, understandably, plenty of interest in an expert who doesn't charge a fee. The website explains that this is a labour of love, a chance to spend an evening discussing the great man with fellow devotees, and all I ask in return is money for my train fare, a hotel room for the night (three stars or above), plus fifty pounds, cash in hand, to cover sundry expenses. As for my attire, the drama departments I teach in have a large supply of costumes, allowing me to refresh or embellish my appearance as I please. After an overly long period 'resting', I had discovered the perfect stage on which to perform my one-man show. Yet as any actor, great or otherwise, can tell you, the real drama takes place once the curtain has fallen...

By the time I'm on the last of my drinks, it's just her and me. The red-headed barmaid left a few minutes ago with a pointed scowl of rejection. Sorry, my little ginger fox, but it's not your turn; close, but tonight my cigar will be smoked by another. My chosen companion has already made significant strides into her forties, I surmise, but retains most of the beauty she undoubtedly possessed in earlier decades. Being blonde and well-groomed immediately sets her apart from the anorak-wearers that normally make up the female minority of my audiences. I'm happy enough with them if there's nothing better about, but tonight I've struck gold, albeit of the worn, brassy kind. A little too much make-up; bright but not clever. I'll take a punt that she does something undemanding in the tourism industry – a safe bet around these parts. To add a little spice, I'll chance that she dabbles as an artist or a potter in her spare time, and has even secured the occasional local exhibition, despite lacking anything close to the requisite talent.

Without flirtation or formal invitation, she follows as I head up to the room the club has provided for my overnight stay. It's on the smaller side of cosy, but pleasingly furnished, if you ignore the framed prints of those wretched hills. The room loses a mark for the kettle, which I can tell simply by looking will never fit under the bathroom tap, yet swiftly gains one for the small porcelain jug of fresh milk sitting alongside, a welcome change to those ghastly little pots of UHT filth. A further mark awarded for the cellophane-wrapped plate of local gingerbread in place of the standard twin pack of custard creams. A nice touch, if a little twee; but then Grasmere never misses a chance to demonstrate that it considers itself a cut above its Lakeland neighbours.

My guest asks if she can use the shower, and I consent. An upward flick of one eyebrow suggests it was an invitation rather than a request, but I'm not a fan of that sort of caper. In my increasingly broad experience, hotel showers are barely large enough for one naked body, especially in old buildings such as this. No, a comfortable double bed with the lights dimmed is my theatre of choice.

As the hum of the water jets bursts through what is evidently an MDF wall, I smoke a cigarette. They always taste so much better when enjoyed beneath a sign that expressly forbids them. The evening is shaping up formidably, and we haven't yet got to the best bit. The dapper, mysterious stranger act has proven, on many joyful occasions, to be irresistible to all types of women. How many? I don't keep a tally. What matters the most is that I enjoy myself hugely and it doesn't cost me a penny, given how few of those I possess. I lean back against the pillow – too firm, half a mark deducted – and await my freshly cleansed acquaintance.

Nothing this good can last for ever, of course, and I always knew it would end eventually. I just didn't expect it to happen at six-fifteen in the morning. After a second, more persistent, rap at the door, I unentangle myself from my bedfellow and open it.

'I'm terribly sorry to disturb you, sir, but there's a slight problem at reception.'

The bellboy, night attendant, whoever he is, doesn't look as if he's sorry. I rub my eyes slowly to indicate that this had better be urgent to justify disturbing me at such an ungodly hour.

'There's a gentleman downstairs who says that his wife is here. With you.'

We both glance at the bed. She isn't visible from beneath the crumpled mountain of duvet, but the dress lying over the back of the chair means there is little point trying to deny her presence.

'I'm sure there's been a misunderstanding,' I smile. 'She told me she was single.'

'Of course, sir, but I'm afraid the gentleman is very insistent. The manager asked me if you'd come downstairs to help resolve the matter.'

'OK. Can you give me five minutes to make myself a little more presentable?'

'Of course, sir, and I'm very sorry to trouble you.'

I smile in acceptance of this second insincere apology, then softly close the door. Swiftly, I pull on my clothes and gather up my collection of Wainwright's books, and then slip out silently, leaving my sleeping former beauty undisturbed.

This is shaping up to be an emergency, so I locate the small sign identifying the exits pertinent to such situations. The staircase at the far end of the corridor offers an escape via the back of the building, well away from reception and its angry bull. Treading lightly in case of squeaky floorboards, I reach the exit next to the kitchen where the staff are already hard at work. There will be no free breakfast this time; a genuine shame, as the aromas emanating therefrom are sumptuous. And all locally reared, according to the hotel – but then which establishment doesn't claim that these days?

After last night's exertions my hunger is fierce, and I am almost tempted to ask for something to take with me, but the noise of sizzling pans and barked orders fails to muffle completely the bellows of the exceptionally irate husband who is evidently not too far away. Quickly, I rifle through the coats hanging up by the back door and, with no little regret, swap my trench coat and fedora for a light blue jacket and baseball cap. A moment's trepidation as I push down the metal bar to open the back door, but my luck holds: it's not alarmed. With the aid of the beer barrels stacked against the back wall, I leap over and into a side street.

Grasmere's solitary bus stop is unhelpfully located in full view of the hotel's front door. It's too big a risk. Instead, and after many months of avoiding them, I must finally set foot upon those blasted fells. Old Alfred gets to have the last laugh, and indeed he has chosen to double down: a wooden signpost gives the name of my only route away from the increasingly loud marital discord erupting from the hotel. Easedale Tarn via Sourmilk Gill. Time to discover if it really is majestic.

If nothing else, it will provide a fitting farewell to a character I've grown to love. He's been hugely successful, enjoyed by audiences in more ways than one. The finest actors know when it is time to move on, however, and so do the middling amateurs such as myself – a shave this close is fair warning. Garth Winfried-Law must let go of Alfred Wainwright – did you work that one out? Of course you did, bless you – and I must head for pastures new. There's no chance of them tracking me down, as my website contains no address, no email, no phone number. But the Lakes are not as vast as their devotees insist, and the chance of running into another angry husband is increasing with every performance.

Yorkshire appeals with its rich literary history, a plethora of appreciation societies, plus a host of country retreats where I can rest my head alongside that of a comely stranger. As I make my way up the singularly unenchanting Sourmilk Gill, I toy with some possible pseudonyms. Toby Merelin? The unusual surname is a giveaway, unfortunately... wait, how about Jerrie

Thomas? The spelling of Jerrie is a little forced, which could lead to my being rumbled before I've had sufficient fun. Tim J.O. Shearer is more convincing, but the use of two middle initials is somewhat unsatisfying. It feels like cheating, and I've very little time for that sort of thing.

16 Two Hundred and Eighty-Two

Garden

It's quieter outside. He exhales slowly, thankful for a few minutes' respite, a rare moment of peace away from the chaos. Although if he stays out too long, there'll be a pay-off later. His mother-in-law was shovelling birthday cake into the twins with the zeal of a French goose farmer. Birthday cake for breakfast; he'd thought about stopping her, but didn't have the energy. Not at the start of what is inevitably going to be an exhausting day. Another exhausting day. He lies down on unmown grass, hoping to recuperate sufficiently during this brief child-free window to get him through the next twelve or more hours.

The gentle slopes of Box Hill rise up in the near distance. They went up it together a hundred times, but she was never impressed. No visit could pass without a complaint that it wasn't a proper hill. Scotland, that was always her dream. Somewhere in the Highlands. He'd hoped a house with views across to the best that Surrey has to offer would compensate a little. Maybe it did, but not enough.

He sometimes blames himself. More often, he blames her. At times, he blames the writers of the motivational slogans that appear on the mugs she used to collect. *Live Your Life Your Way... Regret The Things You Do – Not The Things You Don't... Your Life Is Your Own – Own It!*

Except her life wasn't her own: it was intertwined with those of three other people, who all now have to manage without her. Through the kitchen window, he hears one of the twins start to cry. She's tired, probably. Or needs changing. Or just pissed off with life after trying it for a year. Her brother joins in, just because. Wanting to stay outside just a moment longer, he waits to see if his in-laws can manage.

He blames the kids, too, at his lowest moments. People warned him that once you have kids, they take over – but he'd never expected it to be so hostile. Work life, private life, sex life, all swept away in a tsunami of toys and washing and shopping and tidying and spilt food and dirty clothes and shitty nappies. He loves them, but two kids is one-and-a-half too many.

Scotland was his dream, too, but that was all it was ever supposed to be. A dream.

The wails crescendo. Reluctantly, he heads for the kitchen. The stench of regurgitated birthday cake hits before he's even inside.

Strath More

A blast of mountain air floods the tent as she unzips the door. She checks the weather, the day's first task for any walker. Ice crystals cascade down the outer sheet like a wind chime. It must have dropped below zero in the night, she thinks, and the morning is still chilly. Leaning out, she absorbs once more the sensation of the wild, then shuffles back into her sleeping bag, not yet ready to renounce its warmth. Half in, half out, she stretches into the porch to light the stove and sits the pan on top – she filled it with water the previous night to avoid a cold early morning dash to the burn. You learn these tricks over weeks in the hills.

Through morning haze the peaks south-westwards interlock, each a little less defined than its neighbour. She's not climbed them all – only those topping the magic mark of three thousand feet – but the others will always be there. The violent rattle of boiling water threatens to dislodge the pan and, lifting it carefully, she first fills her white enamel mug – a reliable companion since that first night under nylon – then adds most of the rest to the plastic bowl filled with instant porridge mix. Apple and cinnamon: her favourite, saved to celebrate this noteworthy morning. A small splash of water is saved for washing up. Pans get cleaner when you use boiling water. She learnt that from a fellow bagger who camped with her on Beinn Narnain. You learn these tricks over months in the hills...

Kitchen

Twelve months and two weeks. That's how long it's been since he went walking. Hart Fell, the first thing you hit in Scotland that counts as a proper climb. He remembers the date exactly: two weeks before the twins were born, which was as late as he thought he could get away with it. His last chance to escape. Later, she had used that trip as justification for her own Scottish getaway. One week, that was what they'd agreed. Time to clear her head, sort herself out, have some space.

On the first Sunday, she had rung to tell him she needed another week. Tell, not ask. She told him the same thing the second Sunday. Then she stopped ringing on Sundays. It's now four weeks since he's heard anything at all. He would ask her parents, but he knows they haven't heard from her either. No news is good news, that's what friends tell him, but it doesn't stop him checking the BBC Scotland website each day. No stories of an accident in the mountains, so far, and no news is good news. Up to a point.

He rubs his shoulder, which aches from the weight of carrying babies all day. He feels old, like one of the people they used to laugh at, maybe even scorn: the ones who talked about mortgages not mountains, spreadsheets not summits. He wishes he could get away, just for a weekend, but it isn't possible, not until she comes back. The twins are still too young to be left alone with grandparents. Or are they? But no, he couldn't do that to them. He can't abandon them as well. He could drive to the Peaks and back in a day, but what's the point? You may as well go for a walk in Ikea. No, it's Scotland or nothing. Always has been.

He knows what she's doing; she's ticking them off. They always promised they'd do it together, and to him that was half the point. But not to her; all that mattered was completing them. Maybe one day he'll get to hear about it. Until then, he must make do with staring at the framed sections of maps that hang on their walls, filling the spaces that most people reserve for family portraits. He looks at them some nights, trying to guess what number she's got to. Which one she might have climbed that day.

Ben Hope

She summits alone, her reward for an early start. She doesn't know what time exactly; since her mobile got soaked, her days have been marked by the sun's movement and nothing more. It never mattered what time she reached the top, only that she did. Once down, she removes the plaster and inspects her heel. It's raw, but not infected. And if it hurts, she no longer notices. The blister has been with her for almost as long as the enamel mug.

Fourteen weeks since she stood at the start of the path up Ben Lomond. Over the days in between, she has climbed 282 mountains of a certain height, and walked many hundreds of miles in between – through glen, forest, and far too many along roads. She hitched when those sections became too demoralising. It isn't breaking the rules; the only rules are the ones she decides for herself. Get up when you wake, eat when you're hungry, walk as far as you want, sleep when you're tired. This is her life now, one lived in the great outdoors. No colleagues, no commute. No paperwork, PowerPoints or pointless emails. No washing, drying, folding, ironing. No play dates, parties or parental chatter. No Twitter, no Facebook, no Instagram. She shared pictures from the first few summits, but soon stopped. What was the point? They were her memories. Why share them with people who hadn't made the same sacrifice?

She misses the twins and wants to know how they are doing. Wants to know they're fine. If she could have two lives, she would spend one with them. But no one gets two. She misses him as well, but not enough. Nowhere close to enough. Solitude isn't as lonely as she expected it to be. As her favourite mug at home said, *'Follow The Herd And You End Up In The Abattoir.'* No, going solo suits her just fine. Too many of her former friends had started to file their lifetime dreams under 'regrets' rather than 'ambitions'. She simply refused to do the same.

Ben Cruachan was the wettest. Ben Nevis the most disappointing, unable to escape the Three Peakers clogging the path. Sgùrr Dearg was the hardest – isn't it for everyone? – and Ladhar Beinn the most exhausting. Ben Macdui, tackled in a mix of sleet and wind, was the closest she came to giving up. On Lochnagar two days later under blazing blue skies, she regretted every single day of her life not spent doing this.

Waiting for her skin to dry sufficiently to hold a new plaster, she looks out across Loch Hope. Another memory to treasure, to store away greedily with everything else she has seen. Stags rutting, eagles swirling, otters fishing. The Northern Lights, briefly and faintly. A frozen waterfall. A snow-swept beach, where for one night she believed she was the only person in this world. And so many mountains. An Teallach, that was her favourite. What a day! The full ridge in one glorious, sun-drenched push, and not a soul nearby: a whole mountain to herself. Nothing could ever compete with that.

But now it's over. Ben Hope is her last. There are no more Munros left to climb. The list is ticked. She's joined the club and her name will be added to the others, if she bothers to write and tell them. It's taken two pairs of boots, an upgrade in tent and sleeping bag, many packets of soup and even more bags of pasta. Twenty-two pub meals of varying quality. Twelve nights in hostels, plus two in hotels when she needed a bath and a boost to the spirits. Eight in bothies, with her name and the date recorded in the bothy books. But all the others have been spent outdoors.

Earth and sky. Night and day. Silence and solitude. Sunset and evening star. Ninety-eight sunrises. Ninety-nine sunsets. Today, it is hitting that sweet spot between pink and blue and orange that is indescribably perfect.

But that's it. There are no more Munros to climb, no hills at all to the north. It's time to start heading south.

Settee

With a long sigh, he sinks into it, exhausted. Children are like a sponge, absorbing every last trickle of his time, energy, money. He loves them, but sometimes, just sometimes, he wishes...

'She'll come back, love. She just needs to get it out of her system.'

He doesn't say anything. There's no need to upset his mother-in-law. And he doesn't want an argument, not even a discussion. All he wants is a drink. With a smoothness borne of practice, he manages to unscrew the lid and pour a generous mug of whisky without waking the sleeping baby.

'She was always wild, even as a girl.'

This he cannot deny. She had seemed so adventurous when they met, even by his own standards. He hadn't expected her passion to last, though. That was his mistake. He'd expected her to settle down, eventually. To grow up. To share the responsibility. *Live Each Day As If It's Your Last.* That was one of her favourite mottos. Now, thanks to her, he lives each day like the one before. Cleaning, cooking, tidying, changing. Filling out forms, paying bills. Saturday mornings, which were once spent walking, are now passed in playgrounds, staring at his phone and wondering how an hour can pass so slowly.

She'll get over it.

She'll miss you all too much.

She'll be back, it's just the baby blues.

She's just making a point.

She won't climb all of them.

She won't be gone for much longer.

You'll be fine on your own.

You're a great dad.

Lots of dads are single parents.

'Where do you think she's got to?' his father-in-law asks.

'Not sure,' he replies. 'She must be nearly finished by now. Probably Sutherland, or on one of the islands.'

'I did Ben More last,' his father-in-law smiles. 'On Mull. Something special to end with.'

'I've not done that one,' he admits. 'We tried, but the rain was too heavy. So it's still on the to-do list. Still on mine, anyway.'

'She'll come back,' repeats his mother-in-law. 'When she's completed them. And when she does, you give her a big hug. I'll give her the talking-to.'

He summons up a weak smile and reaches for the bottle. He can usually squeeze in at least three glasses during the ten-minute gap between his children falling asleep and him doing likewise. Some nights, he wishes she would come back. Others, he wishes they'd never met. But mostly, he wishes he'd thought of leaving first.

Durness

She takes a moment to prepare herself. Climbing 282 mountains suddenly seems so simple: this is the real challenge. Sitting on the grass, she fiddles with her rucksack straps, even though they're exactly as they should be. This is the right decision. She knows it is, but better to take a moment to be sure. If she starts, she won't allow herself to stop.

She tightens her boots, then adjusts the rucksack straps again. There's still light in the day, and it's 11,000 miles all the way around, give or take. She may as well tick off a few of them now. But which way around?

The sun is still showing off as it nudges its way towards the horizon, reluctant to leave the stage.

West it is.

It takes about a year, or so others have told her. Not many have done it, but she met one or two when walking. That's how long you need. She hopes to do it in slightly less.

At last, she's ready to begin this next challenge. Almost. Before setting off, she removes three small photos from her wallet and places them under a stone on the beach. She wishes two of the photos a happy first birthday and wonders if she'll be back here just before their second one.

She readjusts her rucksack straps one final time.

Starts walking.

Acknowledgements

Thank you to Heather, Jo and Rhiannon for making this book a great deal better than it was when I first sent it to them. Thanks also to Aidan for suggesting the book's title, and to Helen for her wonderful foreword.

Thanks to Gordon, Gary, Penny, Mike, Dad, Jane and AJ for their feedback on the early drafts of these stories, and their very useful feedback and suggestions.

And special thanks to Bill for his ongoing encouragement and enthusiasm. I would have given up long ago without his good humour and kind words.

Excerpt from their Snowdonia North map reproduced by kind permission Harvey's Maps, www.harveysmaps.co.uk.

About the author

Tim Woods has been writing about the outdoors for most of his adult life. His work has featured in *Elsewhere: A Journal of Place*, as well as outdoors magazines including *Summit, Trail, TGO, Country Walking, The Dalesman* and *Scottish Mountaineer*. Tim is also a co-founder of carfreewalks.org.

Twisted Mountains is his first collection of short stories, drawn from a lifetime spent outdoors. He has climbed mountains all over the UK, and also scaled several of Africa's highest peaks, including Kilimanjaro, Cameroon and Bintumani.

A British-German citizen, he can be found on Twitter **@tim_woods77**.